# Moment of Truth

# SARANORMAL

# Moment of Truth

## by Phoebe Rivers

SIMON SPOTLIGHT
New York London Toronto Sydney New Delhi

SIMON SPOTLIGHT
An imprint of Simon & Schuster Children's Publishing Division
1230 Avenue of the Americas, New York, New York 10020
Copyright © 2012 by Simon & Schuster, Inc.
All rights reserved, including the right of reproduction in whole or in part in any form.
SIMON SPOTLIGHT and colophon are registered trademarks of Simon & Schuster, Inc.
Text by Sarah Albee
For information about special discounts for bulk purchases, please contact Simon & Schuster Special Sales at 1-866-506-1949 or business@simonandschuster.com.
Manufactured in the United States of America 1112 OFF
First Edition 10 9 8 7 6 5 4 3 2 1
ISBN 978-1-4424-6125-3 (pbk)
ISBN 978-1-4424-6127-7 (hc)
ISBN 978-1-4424-6128-4 (eBook)
Library of Congress Catalog Card Number 2012935592

# Chapter 1

A gust of icy wind blew off the ocean and swirled down the back of my neck. I zipped my parka all the way up and pulled my hat all the way down, over my ears.

I had recently moved to New Jersey from California, so this was my first East Coast winter. Freezing-cold weather was new to me. I shivered and hugged my arms tightly. Then I scanned the boardwalk, searching for Lily.

Lily Randazzo was many things: a lively, bubbly, warm person; my first-ever best friend; a member of a big, bustling family that had welcomed me, an only child, with open arms.

But here's one thing Lily was not: punctual.

I leaned against the doorway of Scoops Ice-Cream Parlor and closed my eyes. Thank goodness it was

Friday afternoon. I'd had a lot of trouble concentrating in school all week. I was ready for the weekend.

For the past several nights, a spirit had been keeping me awake. It was the spirit of a sobbing, long-dead woman, who shared the old house I lived in with my father and great-grandmother.

Just one of the spirits, that is.

I've seen spirits since I was a little kid. But last summer, when we moved to Stellamar, I'd started seeing a lot more of them. My great-grandmother, Lady Azura, can see them too. The sobbing woman spirit lived in a room on the second floor of our house. Just next door to my room. She's been there since we moved in, but her weeping and wailing had grown louder and more insistent in recent weeks. I couldn't get much sleep some nights because of it. This week, it had been most nights.

My phone buzzed. A text from Lily.

SORRY! RUNNING BEHIND, WHAT ELSE IS NEW : ) RAN INTO MARLEE AND AVERY! BE THERE IN TEN.

I texted her back. My fingers were numb from taking pictures without gloves on, so I kept it short.

CU SOON.

I pulled out my camera to snap some more pictures while I waited. A jogger passed me. She was running with a large, friendly-looking dog on a leash. It had floppy ears, a feathery tail, and beautiful reddish-brown fur, like a fox.

*Snap-snap-snap.* I took a series of motion shots of them as they passed me. The light was perfect—late afternoon on a late February day, the shadows rapidly lengthening, the sun dipping low in the sky over the ocean horizon.

*Snap-snap-snap.* Until recently, I used to only take pictures of objects. Never people. But lately that had changed. I'd joined the school newspaper as a photographer, and most news stories involved people. I had gotten pretty comfortable shooting pictures of people. One more thing that was different about me now.

So much had changed in the past few months.

I scanned the distant boardwalk with the telephoto zoom lens my dad had given me for Christmas.

Who was *that*?

I lowered my camera and peered at the person making his way toward me along the boardwalk. The wind whipped my long blond hair around my face, and I brushed it back and tucked it behind my ear.

He was still far in the distance. He wasn't wearing a coat. Oddly, he did not seem to mind the cold.

I raised my camera. Zoomed in. Snapped a bunch of pictures of him. He was far enough away that I was reasonably sure he wouldn't think I was taking pictures just of him. As he got a little closer, I could see that he was about my age—maybe twelve or thirteen—and that he was very cute, and tall, with shaggy dark hair.

Then a shock rippled though me. I lowered my camera again and stared at the boy.

He was a spirit.

My first clue should have been the tingling sensation in my foot. My foot always tingles when I encounter a new spirit. Lately it had happened so much that I sometimes didn't even notice it. What gave him away to me was the light. All around him, a light shimmered, and the air sort of rippled as he walked. I watched the jogger and her dog pass him. I snapped another picture. He still didn't seem to have noticed me, so I took a few more.

I hadn't encountered that many spirits my age. Most were old, or at least a lot older than me. I'd have to tell Lady Azura about this. Lately I'd been telling her about all the spirits I saw. It felt good to tell someone. For a change.

Lady Azura was a professional fortune-teller, medium, psychic, whatever you want to call it. She had been communicating with spirits for decades. This was all still pretty new to me. She was helping me to understand my powers. That was one of the main reasons we moved to Stellamar. But my dad hadn't told me she was my great-grandmother until very recently. Just this past Christmas.

The spirit moved closer. He was maybe twenty feet away.

"Boo!"

I must have jumped a foot into the air. I whirled around.

It was Lily, of course. Sneaking up on me to scare me. It had worked.

"I so got you that time!" she said. Next to her were Marlee and Avery, both bundled up against the February chill, both smiling and shaking their heads as if to say they took no responsibility for what Lily did.

5

"Yep, you got me," I said, happy to see my friends. Forgetting all about spirit boy.

"Why are you standing outside? It's, like, seventy-five below zero out here, and you're from California!" Lily exclaimed.

"I was just taking some pictures," I said. "The light is so pretty right now."

"Light, schmight. You artists." She held open the door of Scoops and corralled the three of us ahead of her. The bell on the knob tinkled as we walked in.

"Lily!" yelled the teenage girl behind the counter. It was Dawn Marie, Lily's cousin. Scoops was owned by Lily's "uncle," Paul—not a real uncle, but a close family friend. The fact that he wasn't an actual blood relation of Lily's was unusual. Most of the time, you couldn't throw a rock in Stellamar, New Jersey, without hitting someone who was related to Lily Randazzo. She came from a huge family, with untold cousins, and they seemed to own—or work at—half the businesses in Stellamar.

"What'll it be?" asked Dawn Marie. She didn't look a thing like Lily. Lily had dark hair and big brown eyes, and she was really petite—I had more than a couple of inches on her, and I'm not exactly tall. Dawn Marie was tall, with wavy auburn hair and blue eyes.

"The usual?" Lily asked, turning toward Marlee, Avery, and me. We all nodded. We usually each get the "original" sundae, which comes with two scoops—Dawn Marie gave you extra-big scoops, too. You were allowed to pick two flavors. My favorites at the moment were raspberry chip and chocolate chunk. At Scoops, they put all the toppings on the tables, so you could concoct your own sundae.

After Dawn Marie had handed over our sundaes, and after we'd fished out enough change among us to pay for them and even to leave her a small tip, we made our way to our favorite table near the window.

"So are you pumped for the morp?" Avery asked me, reaching for the chocolate sauce and dousing her sundae liberally.

I looked at her blankly. "The what?"

Avery giggled. "I forget how new you still are! It's the big middle school semiformal. Girls are supposed to ask guys. Morp is 'prom' spelled backward. So it's like a winter prom for the middle school, but with a cool twist."

I looked at her in horror. Nothing about asking a boy to go to a dance with you sounded cool to me.

"They used to call them Sadie Hawkins dances," said Marlee. "Don't tell me they don't have those in California!"

I shook my head. "Not that I know of."

"You don't *have* to go as a couple," Lily explained. "But if you do, it just means you have to invite the guy. And it's sort of dressy, so we have to wear dresses and guys have to wear jackets and ties. But they all wreck it by wearing sneakers. Whatever. The student council is putting up the posters all over the place. It's in two weeks. So are you going to ask Jayden?"

I sat back in my chair. The idea of asking a boy to a dance filled me with dread. Even if the boy was Jayden, who I was pretty comfortable with these days. But I'm definitely not the outgoing type. Think "opposite of Lily," and you get me, Sara Collins.

"I heard Dina talking about it with Caroline Melillo in dance class on Wednesday," Lily chattered on. "Dina told Caroline she's going to ask some cute guy she met at her swim club last summer—Tom something or other."

"Oh, Tom Daly!" said Marlee. "I met him last summer too!" She sighed. "He is sooooo cute. Tall with brown hair and the cutest dimples!"

"Are you going to ask Jack?" Avery asked Lily. Everyone knew that Jack L. had a big crush on Lily.

My phone buzzed with a text from my dad, asking me to pick up some hamburger buns on my way home.

Lily smiled and twirled her dark hair thoughtfully.

I started to text my dad back.

"I'm not sure," said Lily. "Jack is definitely at the top of my list. I'm—" She stopped midsentence.

I heard the bell on the door behind me tinkle.

"Don't. Look. Now," Lily whispered, leaning in toward the three of us. "But the cutest boy I have ever laid eyes on just walked in."

Of course Avery and Marlee immediately looked. I was still finishing my text to my dad, so I was the last to turn around. I hit send and swiveled in my chair.

It was the boy from the boardwalk. The spirit. I whipped around to look back at my friends. They could see him, too! *How was that possible?*

# Chapter 2

I stared at him.

He had his back to us and was up at the counter, ordering a sundae from Dawn Marie. The aura surrounding him was unmistakable. The air shimmered around him. He was a spirit. I was sure of it.

But how could that be?

He was buying ice cream. Paying for it with real money. Interacting with Dawn Marie. Being seen and heard and spoken to. Doing all the things I was sure spirits didn't do. All the things they couldn't do.

I had to be mistaken about him.

"I wonder what school he goes to," whispered Avery.

"He must be new in town," Lily replied. "I know everyone around here. Did you see his eyes? They're green. I looooove that combination, green eyes and brown hair. And he totally looks like an athlete. Just the way he walks you can tell. Sara, can you even believe how cute he is?"

I was barely listening to Lily. The room was spinning. I was wrong about him. I had to be. Spirits don't eat food. Or carry money. Okay, so, the air got shimmery around him. And my foot tingled. Maybe he was just a person with an unusually strong aura, as Lady Azura would say.

If the boy was aware of the fact that there was a table full of whispering, giggling girls behind him, he didn't act like it. He paid for his ice cream and then sat at the counter with his back to us, up on one of the high swivel stools. We were the only other customers in the place. In the summertime, there was a line out the door. But it's not like Scoops does a landslide ice-cream business at the end of February.

"I dare you to go talk to him!" whispered Marlee to Lily.

Avery bounced up and down in her chair. "Yes! I double-dare you! Go ask him if he has any caramel sauce! Tell him we're all out!"

I cringed. *Like we wouldn't just ask Dawn Marie for*

*that,* I thought. But I am clueless when it comes to knowing how to flirt.

Lily shrugged. "Okay, I will," she said easily.

I wished I were more like Lily. She didn't have a shy bone in her body. The prospect of going up to a strange boy, spirit or not, would have given me heart failure. But Lily stood up, tossed her long hair behind her, and strode over to where the boy was sitting.

Avery and Marlee both had a fit of giggling. I half turned to see what was going on. The boy looked up and smiled at her. I watched Lily climb up onto the high stool next to him. The two swiveled so they were facing each other, and were soon chatting away. Well, Lily seemed to be doing most of the chatting. But he seemed more than happy to listen.

"Turn around! Turn around!" hissed Marlee, plucking me by the sleeve. "They're standing up! They're coming over here!"

We pretended to act surprised to see them when Lily and the boy came over to stand next to our table. He was tall—several inches taller than Lily. He wore a Miami Heat sweatshirt and jeans.

"So this is Kyle," said Lily. "He's from Florida: But

he's here with his mom and dad, and they're staying with his aunt and uncle and cousins, who live in
Ocean City. He likes basketball, and he plays for his
school team, but he's not just a lunkhead jock; he had
a pretty big role in his middle school musical this fall."
As usual, Lily managed to fit more information into
ten seconds of speech than anyone I'd ever met.

Kyle chuckled and shook his head as Lily talked
about him. But he didn't seem to mind. "Hey," he said
to the three of us. "Nice to meet you guys."

Lily introduced the rest of us, and we all said hi.
Kyle blurred into and out of focus before me. I had
to hold on to the table to keep from falling out of my
chair.

"This friend of yours, Lily, sure knows how to get a
person to talk about himself," continued Kyle.

"Well, she *is* the school paper's best reporter," said
Marlee loyally.

Kyle looked at Lily. "So she's smart *and* pretty," he
said easily.

Through a hazy fog of nausea, and a roaring
in my ears, I looked at Lily. Was I really and truly
witnessing Lily Randazzo . . . blushing?

I had to focus. I heard the conversation as though through a long tunnel.

"So what are you doing in Ocean City at *this* time of year?" asked Avery. "Most people come here for summer vacation, so they can go to the beach."

Kyle grinned. "My parents are architects," he explained. "And they designed this big new office plaza over in Teabridge. We're staying at my cousins' while they oversee the startup on the construction."

It was so strange, the way the air rippled around him. He seemed so spiritlike. I had to talk to Lady Azura about him, right away.

They prattled away. My gaze moved to the flavor board. I concentrated on reciting the flavors. Chocolate Mousse. Malted Vanilla. Cheesecake Cream. Mango Madness.

My mind cleared. The spinning passed. I felt better.

Kyle glanced at the huge clock over the wall above the door. "Whoops," he said. "I've got to run. I was supposed to meet my parents a few minutes ago. It was great to meet you guys." He made eye contact with each one of us, but his gaze rested on Lily. "Do you come here often?"

"Pretty often," said Lily.

"Cool. Me too. I'll definitely keep my eye out for you from now on."

"Maybe we'll see you again then," said Lily.

"I'd like that," he said, and with another smile and a wave, he loped out of the shop. We watched him head back down the boardwalk in the direction he'd come.

Lily sank into her chair. She raised her chin, passed the back of her hand across her brow, and uttered a dramatic sigh. "Is he not the cutest boy you have ever, ever, ever seen?" she asked us.

We all nodded.

"Dreamboat," agreed Marlee.

"He didn't even touch his sundae," Avery observed. "He was too busy staring at you, Lil."

Lily sat back up and looked at us. "Do you think he might like me? I mean, like-like me?"

"He couldn't take his eyes off you," said Marlee. "Duh!"

"And he practically begged you to come back here so he could meet you again," added Avery.

I knew I ought to say something supportive to Lily. But I was still so shocked by Kyle's spiritlike presence,

I couldn't come up with anything to say. Did Lily notice my silence? She seemed to lapse into a dream state. Staring at nothing, a faraway expression on her face.

"Mar, we have to go too," said Avery, glancing at the clock. She turned to us. "I'm running the scoreboard at the girls' basketball game tonight, and Marlee's doing the stats."

"Have fun," I said.

"Bye, guys!" said Lily, who had managed to emerge briefly from her moonstruck reverie.

After they'd left, she looked at me and sighed. "Wasn't he simply amazing?" she asked, drawing out the "amazing" for about five seconds.

She had asked me a direct question. I had to say something. "Yeah, he seemed pretty great," I said.

She drummed her fingers on the table. I knew that look. She was scheming something. Then she looked at me with a new light in her eyes. "I just had an idea. Come with me to talk to Dawn Marie."

Lily's cousin was drying sundae glasses behind the counter.

"Hey, Dawn Marie, you know that boy who just

left? Has he ever been in here before?" Lily asked.

Dawn Marie smiled. "Who's asking?" she said in a teasing voice.

"I thought it was a simple question," replied Lily, her eyes narrowing in mock annoyance.

"Yep, I've seen him in here a few times," said Dawn Marie. "He always orders the same thing. Sometimes he sits by himself at a table. Sometimes he wanders over to the jukebox and flips through the songs for a while. He never stays long, but he's always nice. And he always brings his stuff over to the bins, and he always leaves a tip."

"Okay, I've got a favor," said Lily, leaning her elbows on the counter. "Next time he comes in here, will you text me?"

Dawn Marie smiled at her. "Of course, cuz. Happy to."

"Thanks, Dawn Marie. I owe you," said Lily.

We bundled back up and headed outside into the blustery cold. As we turned toward home, I touched Lily's arm. "What was that about?"

She smiled. "I might, just might, think about asking Kyle to the dance," she said. "I mean, isn't he to die for, Sara?"

I wished she hadn't used that expression. I swallowed. "Yep, he is really cute."

"I know, right? Let's make a pact. If I ask Kyle to the dance, then you have to ask Jayden."

I shook my head. "I can't. I'm such a coward, Lil. I get all queasy just thinking about asking him."

She smacked her brow, her usual display of exasperation. "Sara. He's a *sure thing*. He's *going* to say yes. Everyone knows he's got a huge crush on you. I mean, he got you a Christmas present, remember?"

I felt my cheeks grow warm at Lily's mention of Jayden's Christmas present. He'd come over a few days before Christmas and given me a pretty blue picture frame . . . and he'd also kissed me. Lily was the only person in the world who knew about the kiss, and I had sworn her to secrecy.

I sighed. I felt myself caving in to her. Lily was my first real friend. I couldn't disappoint her. I was still learning what it took to be a good friend to someone. And besides, there was always the chance Kyle wouldn't come back into the ice-cream shop before the dance. So maybe I could avoid confronting the whole ask-Jayden issue. "Okay, you have a deal. I'll do it if you do."

"Yessssss!" she said. "Now let's go home. I'm freezing!"

We made our way back to our block. Lily and I lived just a few houses away from each other. I remembered to stop at Elber's for hamburger buns, with Lily prattling away the whole time about how cute Kyle was. I did a lot of smiling. A lot of nodding. But I couldn't shake the strange feeling that something about Kyle wasn't quite what it seemed.

The light began to fade quickly. I had to talk to Lady Azura. But when I got home, her door was closed, and it sounded like she had a client in for a reading. She didn't join us for dinner, so it must have been a long and complicated session. I wondered if she'd had to conjure a spirit. She didn't usually do evening sessions for her clients, but I guess someone really needed her help. I would talk to her tomorrow.

# Chapter 3

Saturday. Finally.

At ten o'clock the next morning, I trudged sleepily into Lady Azura's big, sunny kitchen, where my father was listening to the news on the radio. My long blond hair was a mess, and I hadn't been able to find one of my slippers. I'd put on a thick pair of my dad's socks to protect my feet from the drafty floors.

"Morning, Sara," he said, turning down the volume.

I liked the way he looked when he hadn't shaved. He was still pretty handsome, for an old guy.

"They're predicting quite a snowstorm tonight. Eight to ten inches. It figures the winter we move from California, New Jersey gets record snowfall."

I smiled sleepily and lowered myself into a chair. "It also figures it would snow on a Saturday. Plenty of time to clear the roads so we don't miss a minute of school on Monday."

My dad chuckled. "Waffle?" he asked, his ladle poised over the bowl of batter.

I nodded, resting my chin in my hand, my eyelids half-closed. I'd had another rough night of sleep, thanks to the wailing spirit. Last night had been a new low. She'd wailed and wept and moaned on and off all night. I'd tried to sleep with my headphones on, but they kept slipping off and waking me up. And to add to that, something had been wrong with the electricity in the house. I'd awakened several times when my lights had blinked on and off. At 3:12 a.m., I'd been jarred out of slumber when my clock radio had started blasting.

I yawned. "Just how bad does coffee taste?" I asked my dad.

"Trust me. You won't like it," he said, taking a satisfied slurp from his mug. He smacked his lips and shook his head, as though marveling at his own coffee-making skills. "When you're twelve, coffee smells a lot better than it tastes. It doesn't start to taste good until you're well into your teens. And besides, too much caffeine at your age can stunt your growth."

I wasn't sure about the caffeine-growth-stunting thing, but I suspected he was right about the taste. But I was growing desperate. The entire past week, I'd moved through my days like a sleepwalker, exhausted and constantly yawning. I really needed to talk to Lady Azura to discuss what to do about the wailing spirit. Before I stunted my growth from lack of sleep. So that was two things I needed to talk to her about. First Kyle, and then the spirit.

"Rough night last night, kiddo?" asked my dad, clamping down the lid of the waffle iron. I loved when he used his pet name for me.

I nodded. "The house was pretty, um, lively last night. I kept waking up."

He nodded. "Something was definitely strange with the power. My light went on and off a few times. I'm going to check the circuits right after breakfast."

So I guess the wailing spirit wasn't entirely to blame for my lack of sleep. Faulty electricity had contributed. Still, I didn't say anything more about her. My dad couldn't see spirits like I could. Or hear them. But he knew about my powers. In fact, the main reason we'd moved to New Jersey, where my parents had originally met, was that he wanted me to be near Lady Azura, my mother's grandmother. He thought she could help me deal with my powers.

"Did you go out anywhere fun last night?" I asked my dad, eager to change the subject.

He shrugged. "Just a business dinner with the people from the regional office. It was a pretty dull crowd, actually, but the food was good. And, uh, by the way?" He lifted up the waffle-iron handle, and curls of steam spiraled from the perfectly browned waffle. "Just so you know—Janelle and I have decided we're better off just friends. It was a mutual decision. I know you and Dina have had a difference of opinion about us, so I thought you should hear it from me."

"Oh, okay," I said awkwardly. I wasn't sure what else to really say. Janelle had a daughter in eighth grade at school, Dina Martino, and that made things complicated. I liked Janelle fine and all, and I wanted my dad to be happy. I mean, it had been almost thirteen years since my mother had died, giving birth to me. What made it complicated was that Dina was unhappy with the idea of her mom dating *anyone*. Her parents had gotten divorced pretty recently. She'd also decided that I wasn't her favorite person in the world. I tried not to take it personally. She wasn't exactly my favorite person either.

I yawned again. Rested my cheek on the table. My hair tumbled down over my face, but I was too sleepy to brush it out of the way.

My dad, always more of a morning person than me, scuffed merrily around the kitchen in his battered old slippers, whistling tunelessly as he forked the waffle onto my plate and then ladled more batter into the waffle iron. My dad isn't the greatest cook in the world, but he does make a mean waffle.

"I doubled the batter," he said, "in case Lady Azura happens to appear."

We shared the kitchen with my great-grandmother, who lived on the first floor. My dad and I lived on the upper floors. Although recently, we'd been spending more and more time downstairs, ever since I'd learned she was my great-grandmother.

Lady Azura rarely emerged before eleven in the morning, sometimes noon. She was a late-night type. And it took her hours to "put on her face," as she called it, and get herself dressed.

But this particular morning was different. Only a few minutes later Lady Azura stepped into the kitchen, fully dressed and made up. I had just lifted my head off the table and was tucking into my steaming waffle when she emerged from her rooms.

"Do I smell waffles?" she asked in her low, dramatic voice. She stood in the doorway, one arm leaning against the doorjamb above her, the other hand on her hip. She didn't show up so much as she Made an Entrance, like an actress on a stage.

For such a small woman, Lady Azura definitely commanded the attention in a room. She had put on a long, peacock-blue dress, loose-fitting, but cinched in at her tiny waist. Her dyed mahogany hair was swept back into a dramatic twist near the top of her head. On her feet were high-heeled mules decorated with puffy blue feathers. I marveled at her still-delicate feet, the toenails painted an iridescent green. I mean, the woman was well past eighty. I remember the first time I saw her, when we pulled up to the house for the first time. I thought she was totally weird-looking. Now when I see her, I think she looks pretty great.

Lily's always saying what great style Lady Azura has. I don't know much about style, but I think Lily's right. I sometimes wonder if I'll ever be really fashionable like that. Probably not.

I was relieved to see her. I hadn't realized how eagerly I'd been waiting to speak with her privately until I saw her. All my unasked questions about Kyle seemed to bubble up inside me.

"Good morning, Lady Azura!" said my father cheerfully. "The kettle's just boiled and is ready for your tea."

"You don't say," she said drily. "That kettle whistles louder than the five fifty-seven express."

I wasn't sure what that meant, but then, I frequently didn't understand what she meant. Lady Azura was full of puzzling statements. But my dad chuckled.

"I have a waffle cooking that has your name written all over it, if you'd like it," he said.

Lady Azura nodded approvingly. She was never one to say no to sugar. "I always welcome an excuse to douse my plate with maple syrup," she said.

My father poured hot water over her Earl Grey tea bag, which he had put into her favorite cup. He set down her tea and then held a chair for her.

She nodded to him in her queenly way and sat down.

I watched her daintily scoop one, two, three teaspoons of sugar into her cup.

Soon the three of us were sitting around the table, talking and laughing and eating waffles. Just like a regular family. I polished off three waffles, a new personal record for me.

"Sara, you look tired," remarked Lady Azura, setting down her fork and gazing at me intently. Those eyes. They seemed to miss nothing.

"Yes, I—had a lot of trouble sleeping last night." I gave her my best meaningful look, trying to let her know I needed to talk.

The look worked. On my dad, too.

He looked from me to Lady Azura and stood up from the table, dabbing his mouth with his napkin. "Looks like the two of you need to talk," he said, reaching over to collect our plates. "I'll go upstairs and get dressed, and then I'll wash up. Why don't you go have a chat?"

I smiled gratefully at him. I knew he felt a little at a loss when it came to talking about my powers. This was new to both of us. But I was glad I had Lady Azura to talk to, and I know he was too.

Lady Azura nodded. "Come," she said, and led me out of the kitchen. We headed down the narrow hallway and through the purple velvet curtains that marked the entrance to her fortune-telling room. I was once again impressed by how steadily she was able to move on her high heels, which clicked faintly on the faded wooden floorboards.

I breathed in the spicy smell of cinnamon as we sat down at the round table, overlaid with a red brocade tablecloth, in the center of the room. Although the sun was up, the curtains were almost fully closed, casting a dim, rosy light. A narrow beam of sunshine peeking through the drapes glinted off the cut crystal of Lady Azura's summoning bell, making red sparkles dance on the walls.

Lady Azura settled back in her chair and regarded me closely.

I waited. Would she speak?

Her brown eyes were ringed with dark lashes. I'd seen her without her makeup on, so I knew they were false. I felt half-hypnotized, as though I might fall into the brown pools of her eyes.

She wanted me to start. That was clear. I looked around the room and realized that the large mirror that was usually hanging on the wall was gone. "What happened to the mirror?" I asked her.

Lady Azura waved her hand as if to dismiss my question, though after a moment she replied simply, "It broke last night."

"Uh-oh! Isn't that bad luck?" I didn't always believe in stuff like that, but a broken mirror sounded like really bad news to me.

Lady Azura shook her head. "That's nonsense. We make our own luck, my child."

"But how did it break? Was it during your reading last night? You had a client in here, right? Is that when—"

Before I could finish, Lady Azura cut me off. "Sara, you indicated in the kitchen that you had something important to talk to me about. Please tell me what it is."

I studied her for a moment and decided that if she wasn't worried about bad luck, then I certainly shouldn't be. I cleared my throat and began. "Okay. I have a question. About a boy. A boy I met." I fell silent.

"Go on. What is it? I sense *many* questions."

"Yes, Lady Azura, I—"

Suddenly we heard a shrill noise. It was coming from upstairs, almost directly above us. A smoke alarm.

My father yelling for me. A thundering of footsteps.

And then I smelled it. The distinct, acrid smell of smoke.

# Chapter 4

Lady Azura hadn't been upstairs in years, so I didn't wait for her.

I took the stairs two at a time. As I got to the top, I was just in time to see my dad race into the bathroom, trailing a pink curtain that billowed with gray smoke. I followed him down the hall, covering my ears to block out the screeching smoke alarm. I coughed as I inhaled the smoky air.

I stood at the doorway and watched him turn the shower on to douse the clump of charred curtain he'd thrown into the tub. Then he pushed past me and ran back into the pink bedroom. It was the room that was inhabited by the crying spirit.

A few seconds later the sound, thankfully, stopped. I hurried to the doorway of the bedroom. He was standing on a footstool, fanning the air beneath the smoke alarm with an old magazine.

We looked at each other in the sudden silence. I coughed. Then I said, "What happened?"

He stepped down from the stool and went over to the window, which he opened a crack. A chill immediately swept through the room. I shivered and hugged myself. I could still see traces of smoke hanging in the air. The rocking chair moved back and forth, ever so slightly, stirred by the breeze that ruffled the one remaining curtain of the window he'd just opened.

"The curtain caught on fire! May have been the wiring in the sconce near this window," he said, gesturing to an old-fashioned fixture that hung from the wall near the window. It was an ornate brass curlicued light base.

I imagined in the old days, before electricity, it might have held a gas light. Now it had a small electric bulb.

"I was just about to head down to the basement to check the circuit box when I smelled smoke," my father continued. "And then the alarm went off. When I came in here, the lights were all on in the room. There was something strange going on with the circuits last night for sure. Either it's faulty wiring, or the curtain blew back against the bulb and caught fire."

A worried chill eddied down my spine. I looked around the room. I didn't see the sobbing spirit in here now. But I felt her presence. As though she'd been here very recently. I looked up to see my father studying me. "What is it, Dad?"

"I'm wondering how much of an accident this was," he said slowly.

I didn't like the look in his eyes.

Lady Azura stood at the bottom of the steps waiting for us with a troubled look as we descended a few minutes later.

I explained about the curtain catching fire.

"I'm glad you were here," Lady Azura said to my father. "This is an old house. It needs a thorough check of the wiring."

My father nodded grimly. "Yes, it *was* a good thing I was home. It could have been a real disaster," he said. "I think you and I should have a talk."

He glanced at me, and then back at her. I saw them

exchange a look. The look adults give each other that means, *We'll talk later, after the kid is out of earshot.*

I saw his jaw clench up. Noticed the frown lines between his eyebrows. "Right now I'm going down to have a look in the basement at the circuit panel." He pushed past us and headed for the basement.

"Lady Azura," I said, "what is wrong with my dad? Why does he act like he's mad?"

"He's just distressed about the fire. It was a freak accident. Nothing to worry about. I've lived here for decades and have never had any serious problems." She waved her hand dismissively. "Come. Join me in my parlor."

I followed her, still uneasy. We sat facing each other on either end of her deep, luxurious settee.

All thoughts of asking about Kyle fled my mind. I could still smell the smoke. My hair smelled of it.

"What if it wasn't the wiring, Lady Azura?" I asked. "What if it was . . . the spirit that's always crying? Could she be the one who's making the lights blink? Could she have *set* the fire?"

"Of course she didn't set it," scoffed Lady Azura, shaking her head so quickly, her dangling gold earrings rang like tiny bells. "Or if she did, she did not set it on purpose. I do believe her grief is especially strong right now. It's possible that her aura may be causing some sort of extraordinary power surge, enough to affect the electrical currents in the house."

"So that's why the lights were blinking on and off and stuff last night?"

She nodded. Her expression was serious, but unperturbed.

"I didn't know spirits could do things like that, make lights blink on and off. Is it like the way an opera singer's voice can shatter a glass?"

She smiled. "A bit like that. Grief is a powerful emotion, Sara. A heart can be broken. And unlike a broken mirror, which is essentially useless, a broken heart can still continue to function, just in a different capacity."

I wasn't sure what that meant, but I pressed on, eager to learn more. "Lady Azura, what do you know about her? How is her heart broken? I mean, I've been hearing her crying since we moved in, but it hasn't been this bad. All day. All night. She's been waking me up every night for a week, and she's added moaning and blinking the lights and stuff to her regular crying."

"Yes, I hear her too, although my hearing is not what it once was. I am sure you hear everything more keenly than I do."

"It's also just so sad to listen to her," I said.

"Yes, it is a heartbreaking story," Lady Azura murmured with a sigh.

"Isn't there something we can do about it?"

"Remember what I told you. Positive energy. Bring up the white light. Surround yourself with it. Calmness, self-assurance. It will protect you from harm."

"But what about her? The spirit, I mean? I've tried to talk to her, but she wouldn't listen. Wouldn't even stop crying."

"I fear there is nothing we can do for her. Not to mention that she hasn't asked us for help."

"Can you tell me her story?"

She folded her hands. Looked at me gravely. "I will tell you what I know. She lived in this house over a hundred years ago, in the early 1900s. Her child, a boy of only three, fell ill with diphtheria."

"What's that?" I asked. "It sounds bad."

"Yes, it is very bad. Nowadays they have a vaccine

for the disease, thank goodness, but back then it was very common, highly contagious, and greatly feared. It usually starts in the throat and can make it hard to swallow, especially for a small child."

I swallowed, in sympathy, as I listened. For a moment I thought of Alice, the spirit I had helped who had died of polio. Diphtheria sounded as terrible as polio.

"If a person—usually a child—did not receive proper medication, the bacterial infection sometimes produced a powerful poison. The poison spread through the body and caused serious complications. That's what happened to this child. He could have been cured with a simple antitoxin, but the night that he fell ill, a terrible blizzard struck the entire eastern coastline. It was around this time of year—late February."

"That's weird," I said. "They're predicting a big blizzard for tonight, too."

She nodded distractedly. "Yes, I know. And I believe the spirit senses the change in air pressure. The storm that's brewing is reminding her of that terrible night."

She turned toward the window. I couldn't see her face.

"So then what happened?" I prompted.

"The medicine arrived the next morning, but it was too late. The poor child died during the night."

I thought about the woman and her wailing. I missed having grown up without my own mother and was constantly thinking about her. Wondering about her. But my situation was different. I had never known my mother. And then I realized: Lady Azura had also lost a child. Her only child, my mother's mother. My grandmother, Diana, had been forty-six when she died. My mother, Diana's daughter, was in college at the time.

Lady Azura had to be thinking about her own loss. Losing a child. Relating to the spirit on that level.

I focused on what she was saying.

"The mother, our spirit, was of course absolutely bereft. She spent days, weeks, and then months in mourning. She never recovered from her grief. She died a year later, on the anniversary of her child's death, upstairs in that very bedroom, in the bed where he had died."

I felt a sudden chill and shivered. There was a large, flowery silk throw on the couch. I pulled it around me. It smelled of dust and lilacs.

"Every year at this time, her grief seems to redouble. She cannot move past it. She cannot pass to the other world, the spirit world. This year, I suspect her grief has reached new heights and she can perhaps no longer contain it."

"But I don't understand," I said. "After she died, why couldn't she just go join her son and they could be together again?"

"I wish it were that simple, my child," said Lady Azura with a sigh. She stood up and moved to a chair by the window. She clutched the back of it and stared outside at the sky with its thickening gray clouds.

"Spirits are very complicated, just like the living. And as with the living, spirits make their own choices. This spirit has chosen to remain mired—stuck, if you will—in her misery and her grief. It's as though a great, crushing weight is preventing her from passing on."

"Have you ever tried to help her?"

She turned from the window, her eyes bright. "I don't know what I can do, you see. I cannot restore her child to her. I cannot undo the tragic circumstances of his death. And most importantly of all, she has not asked for my help. Nor yours." Lady Azura's dark eyes bored into me. "We must not meddle with a spirit that has not asked for help."

"But we have to!" I said, throwing off the blanket and standing up. "If she keeps blinking the lights and setting fires, my dad might start to worry that it's not safe for us to live in this house." The thought chilled me to the core. For the first time in my life, I felt as though I lived in a place where I belonged. I had a family. I'd made good friends, Lily especially. I felt like I fit in at school. I couldn't move. I *wouldn't* move.

She patted my hand. "Your father is just taking precautions. He knows I've lived here for decades without any real problems. I have dealt with troubled spirits before. Many times. But—" She paused, pursed her lips. "I believe we can defuse the situation so she stops waking you up at night. You look as though you have been losing sleep, my dear, and heaven knows, we need our beauty sleep! Even someone as young and lovely as you. As I think about it, we *can* try to help her. I have an idea. Wait here."

She moved over to an ornately carved side table that took up almost a whole wall. It was over that table that the mirror used to hang. I realized how much smaller the room seemed without the mirror. Lady Azura took something from the top drawer and then turned and held it out to me. A crystal.

I took it from her and examined it. It was a beautiful shade of bottle green. I looked at her quizzically.

"It's green tourmaline," she told me. "It gives you the emotional strength to deal with difficulty and change. You must gain this strength if you are to help her."

"Thanks," I said, somewhat uncertainly. I pulled out the black cord that I wore around my neck, which had been hanging inside my shirt. I untied it. I added the tourmaline crystal to the others I'd been wearing, the crystals Lady Azura had already given to me. I wasn't sure how strength to deal with difficulty and change would help me help the spirit. But I had learned that it was pointless to try to get Lady Azura to explain. She spoke in puzzles pretty often. Sometimes trying to piece together meaning in what she said was like trying to do a jigsaw puzzle. With pieces missing. And without looking at the picture on the box.

"I can see the doubt in your eyes," she said, her

bright eyes amused now. "It's the right crystal for right now, Sara."

I nodded, fingering the lovely green crystal thoughtfully.

"The next time the opportunity presents itself, go to her," said Lady Azura. "Talk to her."

"What should I say?"

"I cannot tell you what to say. I can only guide you toward your path. Listen to what is within your heart."

I nodded, although I had no clue what she meant. I'd already tried to talk to the spirit. It hadn't worked.

"I sense your father coming up the stairs from the basement," she said. "I'll go talk with him. Reassure him."

"Please do," I begged, hearing the desperation in my tone. "I know he doesn't like to talk about this stuff, but you have to convince him—"

My father appeared in the doorway. I could tell from his expression that he was worried. And scared. I stood up and left the room, clutching the crystal tightly between my thumb and first finger.

As I passed through the heavy velvet curtains that led into the front hallway, it dawned on me that I had completely forgotten to ask Lady Azura about Kyle. I knew I had to have that conversation soon. I was worried about Lily without being completely sure why. I would ask Lady Azura about Kyle later. For now, I had to go and try to find the wailing spirit.

As I climbed the stairs, I wondered about Lady Azura's turnaround. She hadn't wanted to meddle at all with this spirit at first. And now she was encouraging me to help her. Why? Could it be that this grief-stricken spirit made her remember her own dead daughter? That Lady Azura felt a kinship with her? Or was she really worried about what my dad might do? Sometimes it was impossible to know what she really thought.

I turned the glass knob of the door to the pink bedroom. Peeked in. She wasn't in there.

I checked the rest of the upstairs.

But she was nowhere.

# Chapter 5

My father went out to run errands for much of the day on Saturday, and Lady Azura had several clients in a row, so I didn't have a chance to talk to either one of them about their conversation. My father returned with a big bag from the hardware store. He had some planks of wood under his arm. He grabbed his toolbox and went straight upstairs, into the pink bedroom. I heard the buzzing of a power saw. The clanking of a wrench. The thud of tools as he tossed them into his box. I gathered he was opening up the wall where the fire had broken out in order to check the wiring. I decided it was probably best not to bring up the subject while he was fixing the burned spot in the room. But I was worried.

The snow started late in the afternoon and was

coming down hard by dinnertime. I thought about calling Lily. I could arrange to have myself invited over to her fun, noisy house for the evening. But then I reconsidered. Better to stay home and do something about the spirit in the house first.

Dinner was a quiet affair. The three of us seemed lost in our own thoughts as we all sat and ate the spaghetti my dad had made. Twice I cleared my throat to bring up the situation with the pink room. To tell my father there was no need to worry. But I stopped myself and stayed quiet. Maybe he would just forget about it. Or Lady Azura would calm his fears.

After dinner I did the dishes. Then I busied myself in my craft room all evening, working on a collage and watching the snow on my windowsill quietly pile higher and higher.

The spirit seemed to have grown suddenly quiet. I didn't hear her at all as I got myself ready for bed that night. But it was an ominous kind of silence.

That night I slept badly again. I dreamed I was trying to run through thick, swirling snow, practically blinded by the whiteness, my nightgown whipping around my legs and tripping me up as I tried to move my feet. I heard the screech of brakes, the shattering of glass, and a terrible thud, which jolted me off my feet, flinging me into deep snow. I clawed frantically at the snow. Gasping for air. Trying to move it away from my nose and mouth so I could breathe. And then I heard a woman screaming.

My eyes flew open. I was grabbing at my pillow, which I had half wrapped around my face, as though in my sleep I'd been trying to muffle my ears to block out sound. I pulled my pillow away and scrambled to a sitting position. Wide awake. Listening. Despite the constant draft blowing from my window, which rattled the shade and billowed the curtains, my body was sweating. It was the spirit that had awakened me.

There they were again. Wails. Shrieks. Moans. They sounded as though they were coming at me from all around, as though the very walls were weeping. The lights flickered on and off. I had never heard her this upset. Was it possible my father could hear her too? Well, even if he couldn't, there was no mistaking the electricity going on and off.

The clock blinked: 2:17. Then it went dark. I flung off my covers and swung my legs out of bed. The floor was icy cold. I still couldn't remember where I'd put my slippers. But I didn't care. I was determined to find the weeping spirit and talk to her.

I could hear the wind howling outside. My shade was half-closed, but I could see that at least six inches of snow had accumulated on the ledge outside my window.

As I opened the door to my bedroom and looked down the shadowy hallway, I heard the weeping diminish somewhat. Strangely, it seemed louder in my bedroom, even though I knew that she was in the pink room. I could hear the rocking chair creaking back and forth, back and forth. I stole down the hallway the few steps to the door and opened it.

She was there, as I expected. I could still smell smoke from the fire earlier in the day, although it was fainter. I could make out the place in the wall near the window where my father had been working. It was patched back up, but a big square of wallpaper was missing, replaced with white spackly stuff.

The spirit was sitting in the rocking chair, her thin arms crossed over her stomach as though it hurt, her head bowed so her long hair tumbled over her shoulders, hiding her face from me. Back and forth, back and forth went the chair. A luminous mist shimmered around her.

As I moved quietly across the room, I could hear the wind outside spring up, whistling through the eaves. Icy snow pattered on the windowpane, which rattled with another gust of wind.

I stopped in front of the spirit. I wasn't sure what to do, so I just stood there quietly. I sensed that she was aware that I was there, but she didn't acknowledge me. She seemed too lost in her grief.

"I'm Sara," I said finally. "Excuse me? Excuse me? I wanted to say—"

*BAM!*

I jumped about a foot off the ground and then whirled around to look behind me to see what had caused the noise. The door behind me had flown open into the hallway, banging against the wall of the corridor. I turned back to look at the weeping spirit. She had vanished.

My father appeared in the doorway. His curly hair was sticking out in several places. His T-shirt was inside out and backward.

"Sara!" he said, rushing into the room. "What are you doing in here? Are you okay? Are you hurt?"

"Hi, Daddy. I'm fine. I just woke up. I, um, thought I heard a noise," I said.

He breathed a sigh of relief and stared grimly around the room, as though searching for trouble spots.

"The power is off," he said.

"I know. I don't think it's because—" I began again. "I think it's due to the storm, Daddy. Look outside. The power is out everywhere. Not just our house."

He glanced out the window, but I don't think he looked very closely. "Go back to bed, kiddo," he said, putting an arm around me. "There's an extra blanket in the chest at the foot of your bed. It might get pretty cold in here by morning if the power stays off."

I nodded and slipped past him, eager to get back under my covers. I saw him take one more look around, and then close the door of the room and walk back toward his own.

The next morning, Sunday, dawned bright and sunny. I'd awakened twice more in the night but hadn't been sure what had woken me. I didn't hear more wailing. But I'd heard *something*.

It was freezing in my room. My clock was off. The power must have still been out. I heard the sound of my father shoveling outside. I climbed out of bed and peered out of my window. The snow was heaped and swirled like the top of a lemon meringue pie. By the looks of the dim sunlight, it seemed to be midmorning. I'd slept late, for me. I could see that my father had nearly finished shoveling the walkway and the area in front of the garage. In the distance, I heard the rumble of a snowplow.

Downstairs in the kitchen, by the battery-operated clock over the sink, I saw that it was ten thirty. I turned toward the refrigerator to pull out the milk for some cereal and encountered a sticky note in my dad's hand-writing: *DO NOT OPEN!*

Right. The power was off. Had to keep the door closed.

He walked in a minute later with a half gallon of milk, which he'd put outside in a snowbank to stay cool.

"Morning, kiddo," he said, stomping his boots on

the mat and pulling off his gloves. "I think I'll join you for a second breakfast. Shoveling snow really works up an appetite!"

We ate quickly. We didn't talk about what had happened in the middle of the night. As soon as I had finished my cereal, I quickly rinsed our bowls in cold water and then hurried upstairs to bundle up so I could help him with the shoveling.

We came in for lunch. I was hot. Sweaty. My shoulders ached. We found Lady Azura in the kitchen. She had woken up with a cold. Luckily, the gas stove worked. I made her a cup of tea, but she shuffled back to bed and stayed there most of the day. I looked in on her a few times, but she was always sleeping. I couldn't bring myself to wake her up to talk to me. So once again, I missed the chance to ask her about Kyle.

The power came back on midafternoon—just in time to get my homework done.

I plugged in my phone to charge it. Almost immediately it buzzed with a text from Lily.

HEY! IS YOUR POWER BACK ON YET? OURS JUST CAME ON.

I wrote back: YEP. OURS JUST CAME ON TOO.

PERFECT TIMING. NOW WE'LL HAVE SCHOOL TOMORROW.

YEP. GREAT.

I PROMISED CAMMIE I'D HELP HER BUILD A SNOWMAN BEFORE IT GETS DARK. WANNA HELP?

I massaged my aching shoulders. Shoveling snow had made me realize I had muscles I didn't even know I had.

I'M A CALIFORNIA GIRL, REMEMBER? I NEED TIME TO BOND WITH THE WHOLE SNOW THING.

FINE. BE THAT WAY :D

I smiled. It was nice to know Lily never got mad about stuff like that.

By Monday morning the skies had cleared and the plows had been through, and school began right on time. Terrific.

The morning droned on. Finally the bell rang for lunch.

It was such a nice feeling, to walk into the cafeteria without feeling scared. Or worried about where to sit.

I saw Lily jump up from her chair and wave me over.

"We're talking about the morp, what else," she said as I sat down with my tray a few minutes later.

"There's a shocker," I said with a grin. It struck me that I hadn't even thought about what I would wear, if I went. Tamara and Marlee were describing their dresses to each other in minute detail.

"I heard Dina asked Tom Daly from her swim club," said Avery. "And he said yes."

"Have you seen your new crush again, Lily?" Marlee asked excitedly. "Mystery Man from Scoops?"

Lily reached over for one of my chips and popped it pensively into her mouth. She sighed and shook her head. "But it's not like anyone was going much of anywhere this weekend," she said. "Dawn Marie told me they closed Scoops early on Saturday because of the snow, and that yesterday it was closed too. Luckily, they got the generator working so the ice cream didn't melt."

Friday felt like it had happened ages ago. I thought back to when I'd first seen Kyle, walking along the boardwalk. Then I suddenly remembered something. "Hey, Lil," I said. I bent under the table and unzipped my backpack. "I just remembered. I was snapping a bunch of pictures at the boardwalk while I was waiting for you. I think there are some shots of Kyle in here." I pulled my camera out and began scrolling through the picture archive.

*"Why do you have pictures of him?"* Lily said. *"Do you have a crush on him too?"*

I jerked my head up from my camera. "What? No! What are you *talking* about? I don't have a crush on Kyle!" I looked at her. She had a strange look on her face. I looked around the table. Marlee, Avery, Miranda, and Tamara had all stopped talking. They were looking at me like I'd just said something extremely bizarre. I felt my face get hot. I knew I was probably bright red up to the roots of my hair. Had I just imagined I'd heard Lily say that?

My friends gave me one final odd look and then went back to talking with one another. Lily just looked down at her lunch and didn't say anything else.

"Actually, never mind. I was wrong," I said, shoving my camera back into my bag. "I guess I must have accidentally erased the pictures I took that day." I gathered my stuff and stood up, even though there were still ten minutes before the bell rang. "I have to run to the bathroom before science," I said. "See you guys."

I headed for the girls' bathroom nearest to science, which was practically all the way across the school, rather than the one near the cafeteria. I didn't want to risk running into one of my friends from the lunch table, least of all Lily. The truth was, I hadn't erased the pictures from my camera. They were all there. But there was something very wrong with them. I needed time to look more closely.

I put my bag on the counter and pulled my camera back out. Then I scrolled carefully through the pictures I'd taken the previous Friday. There was the jogger and her pretty, reddish-colored dog, running by me. And then past me, in a series of motion shots. There was the sun, dipping low in the sky over the horizon, above the choppy gray water. And there. That should be Kyle, walking toward me along the boardwalk, just as the jogger and her dog were passing him on the left.

*But there was no Kyle.*

Where he had been, where he *should* be in the picture, there was nothing. Nothing but empty space.

# Chapter 6

"Collins!"

As I emerged from the girls' bathroom, I heard the booming voice. Bellowing all the way down the still-empty hallway.

I groaned inwardly. It was the same spirit I'd come across a few months ago in the school cafeteria, back when I was the new kid, trying to fit in at my new school. That had been the first time I had actually had a conversation with a spirit. Why did my first spirit conversation have to be with *this* spirit? A big, loud, obnoxious gym teacher who had serious boundary issues? And why did my first encounter have to happen in the middle of a crowded school cafeteria?

Ever since that first conversation, he had been coming and going, bothering me on and off. He seemed so psyched that I could see him. The last time I'd seen him, he told me he needed me to do him a favor. He wanted me to deliver something. I had ducked out of his sight. Now I spent a lot of time trying to avoid him.

"Collins! Need you to deliver something for me. Collins! Collins! Listen. Okay, never mind. Got a good one for you!"

Oh yeah. He also liked to tell jokes. Bad ones.

He charged down the hallway in my direction. "What's big and yellow and arrives in the morning to brighten your mother's day?"

I pretended not to hear him.

"Give up? The school bus! Get it? You thought I was going to say 'the sun,' but that's the joke, see."

I continued to look everywhere but in his direction. For a whole lot of reasons, I didn't find his joke funny. His polyester tracksuit looked so . . . old-school, in the brightly painted, modern hallway.

"I got a favor to ask you, Collins!"

The bell rang, and the hallway filled up with kids hurrying to their lockers and their next class.

Then I had a sudden thought.

As he made his way toward me through the

increasingly crowded hallway, I pulled my camera out. I watched him stop and stare indignantly at a couple of boys walking away from him.

"Tuck in those shirts!" he yelled after them, but of course, they ignored him. "Kids these days!" he said, shaking his head and waggling his thick gray eyebrows.

Quickly, while he wasn't looking my way, I snapped a picture. Then another one.

"Collins!" He seemed to remember I was there. "I need you to deliver something for me! Collins! Come back here!"

But I managed to avoid him. I ducked around the corner and then moved quickly down the hall and into science.

The second bell had not yet rung, and people were still coming in and getting out their stuff. While Miss Klingert passed out the day's labs, I peeked at the pictures I'd just taken in the hallway.

My instincts had been right.

There was the crowded hallway, the two boys with their untucked shirts. The poster advertising the morp dance next Saturday. But where the gym teacher spirit's image should have been, there was empty space.

Now I knew.

It was no coincidence that Kyle hadn't appeared in the pictures I had taken last Friday.

Kyle had to be a spirit.

I had to talk to Lady Azura about him right away.

But then I forgot all about Kyle, because Jayden passed by my desk. At first he pretended not to see me. I pretended not to notice. Then he stopped, turned, and playfully kicked the sole of my sneaker with his big high-top.

"You going to sit there, staring into your backpack all class?" he asked.

I smiled and put it on the floor. "I find the contents endlessly riveting," I said. "My textbooks never cease to fascinate me."

"Well, here's something that will fascinate you— our alloys lab. Here. Take your goggles."

He tossed them to me, and I caught them neatly with one hand.

"Thanks," I said.

He nodded approvingly. "I only work with lab partners who have good hand-eye coordination," he said.

All during the lab, I tried to screw up the courage

to bring up the morp but couldn't find a way to work it into the conversation naturally. And, if I'm being really honest, I chickened out.

After science, I had social studies with Mr. Blake. Lily slipped into the desk next to me just as the second bell rang.

"Nice work, Lily," said Mr. Blake with a wry smile. "I'm very proud of your newfound efforts at punctuality. You've been on time two days in a row now."

Lily smiled sweetly at him. "Working on it, Mr. Blake!" she said with a giggle, and pulled out her notebook.

As she opened it up, I noticed she'd doodled the name "Kyle" all around the margins of her notes.

"We'll be working on the colonialism maps with partners today," Mr. Blake said as he passed out some oversize papers.

"Partners?" Lily immediately turned toward me.

I felt a flood of relief. I wasn't sure if she was still mad at me about what had happened at lunch. "Partners," I said. We scootched our desks together and pulled out our colored pencils.

I was coloring in the Gadsden Purchase of 1853 when Lily nudged me with her elbow. "Hey," she said under her breath. "I was thinking about walking home after school by way of Scoops. You know, to check out the scene. Dawn Marie texted me to say she'd be working today, so I thought, maybe, if Kyle shows up, we could go there together?"

"I'm sorry Lil, but I can't," I said weakly. "I—I have to get home. I promised." How could I explain to her that I was blowing her off in order to try to help her? I had to get home to Lady Azura and ask for advice about how to deal with Kyle. I stared down at my map, not wanting to meet her eye.

*"You don't want me to find him, obviously. You must like him yourself. I thought you liked Jayden."*

I looked at her quickly. But she wasn't talking to me, or to anyone. She was staring down at our map, her chin in her hand, dolefully coloring in the Louisiana Purchase. Had she said that out loud? Had she just *thought* it and I'd somehow . . . *heard* her?

"Okay, that's cool, whatever," she said. Out loud this time.

We didn't say much more to each other for the rest of the class. Then the bell finally rang.

# Chapter 7

I found Lady Azura in the kitchen when I got home from school that afternoon. She was drinking what looked like tea from a delicate china cup. No doubt with three heaping teaspoons of sugar stirred into it. She had set out a plate of ginger cream cookies—a new favorite cookie of mine that Lady Azura had introduced me to. It was almost as though she'd been expecting me. She had a knack for knowing when I'd show up.

She and I hadn't talked much about the sobbing spirit, but the tension in the house was high. All weekend my dad had been moody and distracted, and he had spent a lot of time on Sunday setting up his stepstool beneath all the light fixtures in every room, unscrewing things and peering into sockets with a flashlight. I guess he was worrying about the wiring.

"How is your cold?" I asked.

"Much better, thank you," she replied. And she did look better. "I always drink an herbal concoction with fresh ginger, honey, and lemon that works like a charm."

I sat down, took a cookie from the plate, and got straight to the point. I told her about seeing Kyle on the boardwalk. About thinking he was a spirit. About how my friends could see him. About how he didn't show up in the photographs. "He is a spirit, right?" I asked her.

Lady Azura set down her teacup and nodded. "It seems so, yes."

"Then how come other people can see him? I don't understand."

She picked up her cookie, broke it into two neat halves, and then set it back down on her saucer. "I believe you have met a spirit who doesn't know he is dead," she said. She pulled a lace handkerchief from her sleeve and daintily blew her nose.

I raised my eyebrows but waited for her to continue.

"It is a very rare phenomenon," she went on, "something I've heard about but have never before encountered. But as I understand it, such a thing happens if a person dies suddenly, before his time. His spirit doesn't know—or can't accept—what happened. The person's energy is so strong that his spirit is somehow able to walk around on earth temporarily as though he is alive. He has no memory of what happened to him. My guess is that Kyle must have died suddenly, perhaps violently."

I shivered. "You said temporarily. How long will he be in . . . this state of not knowing?"

"I don't know," said Lady Azura. "As I said, I have never witnessed this phenomenon myself. My guess is that he will remain this way until he finds out the truth somehow. And when that moment comes, it could be very difficult for him, and for anyone who happens to be near him."

"Like me," I said. I hadn't told her about Lily's crush on Kyle.

"Yes," she said, nodding. Then, more to herself, she murmured, "That poor boy."

"But if he is really and truly a spirit," I ventured on, "then why does he order ice cream? Evidently he orders it all the time when he goes to Scoops. Can a spirit eat?"

"There are no hard-and-fast rules when you are talking about the spirit world," said Lady Azura. "Because Kyle believes he is alive, he probably believes he needs to eat. He may order food in a restaurant, but his body has no corporeal need for food. He has no hunger because he has no earthly body. I suspect the realization will occur to him soon, if he continues to interact with you. And with your friends."

Again, that penetrating look. Did she somehow know about Lily? That wasn't possible. Was it? Of course it was. Lady Azura seemed to know everything.

"Sara," she said, leaning across the table and staring at me intently, "I want you to be very, very careful with this spirit. Stay away from him. Finding out the truth will be difficult for him. I don't believe he is a malevolent spirit, any more than I believe our upstairs spirit is malevolent. But it seems only a matter of time before the realization hits him, and he could react violently. This goes beyond the reach of what you can do to help. You must stay away."

I thought about Lily. What about Lily? If I didn't help, she could be in real trouble. I opened my mouth to say something. But she shook her head.

Conversation over. I closed my mouth.

"Now that we've discussed that situation, there is something else I wish to talk to you about."

"My dad?"

She nodded. "I sense that your father is deeply troubled about what happened upstairs the other day. Of course, he is concerned for your safety. His fears are understandable, if unfounded. He has lost enough."

I sat back in my chair and stared at her. "But you explained to him that the crying spirit didn't set the fire on purpose, right?" I heard myself talking, but I wasn't even sure what I was saying was true. What if she *had* set the fire on purpose?

Lady Azura flicked her handkerchief, a kind of scoffing motion. "I explained to him that this is an old house, and that it has been standing for a very long time. I am sure he is worrying unnecessarily. I sense he may just be having a stressful time at work. Your father absorbs stress like a sponge, Sara. I have no doubt that together you and I can convince him his fears are unfounded, that we are in no danger."

Yes, I would do that. No matter what I really thought—that maybe the spirit *was* doing this on purpose—I would convince my dad it was nothing. Because what if he got so freaked out he wanted to move? The thought of leaving the house was too awful to contemplate. Not now. Not ever.

I stood up from the table. "I'll convince him," I said. "I have to. And I'll start by getting the crying spirit to talk to me, and to stop messing around with the electricity. But Lady Azura, I don't understand why I can't also talk to Kyle. You said yourself that he doesn't know he's not alive. So how can he ask for help if he doesn't know he needs it?"

Lady Azura's eyes grew steely. I hadn't seen this expression on her face before, at least not directed at me. This tough-as-nails, I-can-bend-a-fork-with-a-look side of her. She did not want me doubting her judgment. That was clear.

"The crying spirit is here, in our house, where I can protect you if you encounter danger. But Kyle is an unpredictable force. I want you to stay away from him, Sara," she said in a firm voice. "No buts. Do as I say."

We stared at each other, but of course I looked away first. I nodded quickly, swept up in her force field.

It wasn't until afterward, when I'd left the kitchen

and was heading upstairs, that I was struck with a sudden realization: I had to help Lily. And I couldn't tell Lady Azura anything more about my dealings with Kyle.

My phone buzzed. I glanced down at it. A text from Lily.

HE'S THERE! AT SCOOPS! RIGHT NOWWWWWW!! CAN YOU GET AWAY? MEET ME AT THE CORNER?

I texted back: BE RIGHT THERE.

# Chapter 8

Lily was waiting for me when I got to the corner. She was all bundled up and scuffing her feet impatiently, like a racehorse waiting to be released from the starting gate. That had to be a first. Lily had *never* gotten anywhere before me. All my fears about whether she was mad at me vanished when I saw her smile at me as I approached.

"Thanks for getting away," she said, linking her arm through mine. "Hope I didn't get you in any trouble at home."

"No, it's all good," I said casually, hurrying to keep in step with her as we turned onto Beach Drive. "There were just a few things I had to do for Lady Azura."

"Dawn Marie says he just showed up. Do I look okay?"

I smiled. "You look awesome."

And she did. Beneath her open coat she wore a bright pink chunky sweater and skinny jeans. And a bunch of silver necklaces. Lily was born with all the fashion sense that I lack. Which is probably why she and Lady Azura got along so well.

She pulled me back as we were about to pass by the window of Scoops, and we stopped. "Okay," she said, pulling off her hat and smoothing her hair. "Here's the drill: We go in. We pretend not to see him. Then we wait to see if he remembers me and says anything. If not, I'll pretend to, um, notice him and reintroduce myself. Sound good?"

I nodded, trying to ignore the apprehensive shivers winnowing down my spine.

Dawn Marie was just handing Kyle his sundae when the bell tinkled as we entered. Kyle didn't turn around.

"Hey, cuz!" said Dawn Marie cheerfully. "What'll it be today?"

Kyle swiveled around. He seemed to recognize us instantly. He hopped down from the stool at the counter and waved, looking directly at Lily.

"Hey!" he called, and broke into a broad smile.

The way the air shimmered around him was unmistakable. He seemed to glow brightly and then fade. Did he really look totally normal to Lily? This was so confusing. Next came the prickly feeling in my foot. A wave of nausea. I was glad I was there, to protect Lily in case something went wrong. But my body's physical response to him was not fun. Exactly how I would protect her if something happened, I had no clue. I had to try to find out everything I could about him.

"Oh! Hi!" said Lily in pretend surprise as she guided me toward a table in the corner. "Kyle, isn't it?"

His grin widened. "Yep. And you're Lily." He said her name with a little lilt, as though he'd said it to himself many times. "And, sorry, forgot your name," he said to me, looking genuinely apologetic.

"Sara Collins. What did you say your last name was?" I tried to make my voice sound as neutral as possible.

"Parker."

Parker. Kyle Parker. I made a mental note to look him up later.

The shimmery air, the glowing vision, the tingling

feeling in my foot, all faded. Now I felt almost normal, looking at Kyle. At least now I could focus on the two of them together.

Lily's dark eyes sparkled as Kyle made his way over to our table. He left his sundae abandoned at the counter. I caught a glimpse of Dawn Marie smiling a little as she busied herself organizing long spoons in a drawer. I noticed that Kyle was wearing the same clothes he'd had on last Friday. *Of course. Those must be the clothes he died in,* I thought. *Won't Lily notice he's wearing the same outfit again?*

But Lily didn't seem to notice. Or maybe she didn't care. Kyle sat down. A few seconds went by, and I waited for Lily to say something. I'd never seen her at a loss for words, but this seemed to be a first.

"Sooooo," said Kyle, filling the silence. "Come here often?"

Lily burst into giggles.

I'm not much of a giggler, but I was trying to bend over backward to keep her from getting upset with me. Or thinking I liked Kyle too. So I laughed a little.

We sat there some more. I realized I would have to

step up. Plus, I needed to find out more information about Kyle.

"So, Kyle," I said. "Where are you from in Florida?"

"A small town on the Gulf Coast called Bradenton. I'm sure you've never heard of it, but it's kind of near Sarasota."

"I would love to be in Florida right now!" said Lily, gesturing out the window at the snow that was still heaped up everywhere.

"Yeah, it's pretty great to live there," he said, "especially if you're a baseball player. I play year round. Pitcher and first base. Lefty."

"And what about school?" I asked, trying to keep my tone casual. "Aren't you missing a lot while you're here with your parents?"

"Missing school?" he said, looking a little confused. "Well, no, I'm here on my break, um, for the holiday. And my school will let me make up the time I missed, um, later."

His voice trailed off uncertainly. I glanced at Lily, but she didn't seem to have noticed his confusion.

"How long will you be around?" she asked suddenly.

I knew where she was going with this. She wanted

to find out if he'd be here for the dance. Another wave of nausea rose up inside me. The room began to spin.

"Oh, for a while," he said vaguely. "My parents have more work to do on their big project." Suddenly he looked at the clock over the door. "Speaking of my parents, I gotta go," he said, shoving back his chair. "Supposed to meet them. Hey, Lily, you're from around here, aren't you?"

She nodded. "Born and raised."

He grinned. "Do you mind walking with me and pointing me toward Tidewater Street? I'm supposed to meet them at that corner."

Lily's smile broadened. "Sure. You don't mind, do you Sara?" she asked.

I did mind. What if something happened? Something that made Kyle realize he was a spirit? But it was clear they wanted some time alone together. I couldn't ask if I could tag along. "No, that's fine," I said. "I have to get back home anyway. But text me later, okay, Lil?"

She nodded happily. Jumped up from her chair. We hadn't even ordered anything.

I watched the two of them leave together. Kyle held the door for her. Once again, he had no coat on, but the air had warmed up today, and although there was still a lot of snow, it wasn't all that cold.

"Awww, young love. Right, Sar?" called Dawn Marie from behind the counter. She winked at me and went on with her work. Through the window, I watched them walk away together. The humming in my ears got louder, and the nauseous feeling grew so strong, I was afraid I might throw up. I had to sit there for a minute before it finally passed and I could stand up and leave.

I was so lost in thought as I made my way down Beach Drive that I almost collided with someone who was walking the other way.

"Sorry!" I said, quickly stepping to the side.

"You oughta be!" said the guy angrily.

I looked up quickly, alarmed by his tone.

It was Jayden. He grinned.

I grinned back. My knees went all wobbly. Why did he have such an effect on me?

Jayden stepped on my foot gently, teasingly. It was his little flirty gesture, stepping on my foot. I loved it. "What's up, Sara? Heading home?" he asked. He wore a navy-blue knit hat low down on his forehead. Only Jayden could look that cute in a knit hat. Under one arm he clamped a basketball, and slung over his shoulder, a pair of high-tops.

"Yeah, on my way home from Scoops," I said. "How was practice?"

"Tough. Coach made us run sprints every time someone missed a foul shot. I'm on my way home to consume my body weight in dinner."

Flirtatious conversations with boys were new to me. But I knew it was my turn to say something. It was now or never. Suddenly I felt really brave. I took a deep breath. "So, um, I was wondering."

"Yes?" He looked straight at me, almost like he'd been waiting for this moment.

"Are you—do you—would you like to . . . go-to-the-dance-with-me-on-Saturday?" The last part of the question came out double time. "The 'morp,' or whatever it's called?" I held my breath and then looked up at him. He was smiling.

"I thought you'd never ask!" he said in a funny dramatic drawl.

Relief eddied around me like a wave around a

rocky shore. "So that's a yes?" I asked in a small voice.

"That's a *heck*-yeah," he said, rolling his eyes. "We can talk about timing and stuff later, though. I have to go eat some food. My stomach is starting to digest itself."

I was still smiling as I reached the corner of my block.

As soon as I got home, I ran upstairs to my craft room and opened my laptop. It didn't take long to find the news about Kyle and his parents.

A car crash.

Less than three months ago. Two weeks before Christmas. Suddenly I remembered hearing about it on the local news. There had been a big blizzard that night, quite unusual for that early in December, especially near the coastline. The newspaper article I found online said that Kyle and his parents, John and Cecily Parker, had been driving between Ocean City and Stellamar. Their car had skidded, spun around, and hit an oncoming truck broadside, and the three were killed instantly.

The accident had happened at the intersection of

Beach Drive and Tidewater Street. I realized that was where Kyle had told Lily he was meeting his parents.

I closed my eyes and took a deep breath, thinking about Kyle. It was horrible. But I kept reading. I had to find out everything I could.

The article mentioned that the Parkers were from out of town and were here on business. An aunt, Carla Daly, was quoted as saying they'd been on their way to Stellamar for ice cream. That explained why Kyle kept returning to Scoops.

I suddenly remembered the dream I'd had. Was it just Saturday night, the night of the blizzard? I'd dreamed about screeching brakes and shattering glass and being thrown into a snowdrift. Was that some weird coincidence, or were my dreams somehow a way that spirits were sharing memories with me of past events? Not *my* memories, theirs. It was kind of freaky to think about.

I found another article, this one an obituary. It talked about Kyle's parents and their work. It mentioned that Cecily Parker was survived by a sister, Carla Daly, and a brother-in-law, Edward Daly, who lived in Ocean City, and by two nephews, Thomas and Charles Daly.

My heart skipped a beat. Thomas Daly from Ocean City! Ocean City was not a large town. It had to be the same person as Tom Daly, the boy from Dina's swim club who she had asked to the dance this Saturday. Were Tom Daly and Kyle Parker cousins?

They had to be.

I rubbed my temples, which were starting to pound. If Kyle went to that dance, his cousin Tom would obviously see him. That could be a disaster. A disaster happening in a large, crowded place. What if Kyle dealt with it badly? I'd already seen what kind of damage a spirit could do in my own house, and that was just from sadness. Lady Azura had used the word "malevolent." What if Kyle turned into a malevolent spirit?

Somehow, I had to stop Lily from asking Kyle to the dance.

My phone buzzed. It was a text from Lily.

I ASKED KYLE TO THE DANCE AND HE SAID YESSSSSSS!!!!

# Chapter 9

Later that afternoon, I overheard my father and Lady Azura having an intense, murmured conversation together in the kitchen. I thought about listening outside the door, but I didn't. I entered the kitchen. I could tell by the worried, confused expression on my dad's face, and the deepening frown lines on Lady Azura's, that the two were not exactly seeing eye to eye. I felt sure it was about me. And about whether we might have to move.

"I ordered Chinese," said my father stiffly. "It'll be here in twenty minutes."

I nodded. Feeling miserable. Helpless.

Dinner was a quiet affair again.

Monday night I heard the wailing, crying spirit on and off all night. I'd found some earplugs at Elber's, which helped some, but they didn't stop me from waking up when the lights flickered on and then off again. A couple of times my radio started blasting for no apparent reason. I ended up unplugging it and using my MP3 as my alarm clock. I woke up feeling exhausted.

At school on Tuesday, I couldn't bring myself to congratulate Lily about asking Kyle to the dance. She sensed my ambivalence for sure. Her behavior toward me was cool. We sat together at lunch, and we sat together in social studies, and we talked and worked together and even joked around a little. But it still didn't feel normal. Ever since our brief exchange of texts about how she'd asked Kyle to the dance, we hadn't discussed it. I couldn't seem to find the right time to bring him up. Clearly she was upset that I hadn't been enthusiastic enough about her news. She was right. I *hadn't* been.

The wailing spirit wasn't the only thing that had kept me up the night before. I'd been losing sleep, stressing about Lily. She was my first real friend. I remembered a time not very long ago when I couldn't imagine having a close friend at all. And now I couldn't imagine *losing* her. What would I do if she stopped speaking to me?

My father was becoming borderline obsessed with fire safety. He kept unscrewing outlets and fixtures, checking and rechecking wiring, and peering into the fuse box in the basement. On Tuesday afternoon, he came home from work early with a huge box that turned out to contain one of those collapsible ladders. The kind that you could hook around the window frame of a second- or third-story window, and then toss out and climb down. He put it on a shelf of my closet and made sure I understood how to work it. Then we reviewed—again—the evacuation plan in case of a fire, and where we would convene once outside, and how I absolutely couldn't stop to grab any of my things. I'd learned all that in preschool, but I realized he needed to do it for his own wobbly peace of mind.

Lady Azura seemed to have convinced herself that my father was acting unreasonably. Even though the last thing in the world I wanted to do was admit he had a point, I was bothered by a nagging feeling that she was the one being unreasonable. Something was off in our house. I could feel it. It was almost like we were all just waiting for something to happen.

I was quite sure that she was right, that the wailing spirit didn't *intend* to harm us. But what if her raw, helpless grief took an ominous turn toward rage? What if she became angry at the world for taking her child from her? Then things really *could* turn dangerous. Still, in my heart, I didn't think she meant any harm, nor would she ever. The challenge would be to convince my dad that that was true. And the only way to help her stop making things go wrong in the house was to help her come to terms with her child's death.

Like I had any clue how to help her to do that. I couldn't even get her to talk to me.

Lily and I sat at the same table at lunch on Wednesday. But we didn't sit next to each other. I wasn't sure whether our friends noticed. Most of them seemed completely focused on what to wear to the dance. I couldn't bring myself to really care what I was wearing to the dance. And no one asked me what I was planning to wear anyway.

On Wednesday afternoon I couldn't stand the tension one minute longer. I went to look for Lily. I knew that it was her dance class day and that her mom would be picking her up, so she wouldn't be in a rush to catch the bus. I managed to find her alone at her locker, just after the final bell of the day had rung.

"Lil!" I said, hustling toward her through the throngs of kids hurrying the other way, toward their buses. "Wait up!"

She had just banged her locker shut and was hoisting her sports bag onto her shoulder. "What's up, Sar?"

"I was just wondering. Are you still going to the dance with Kyle, or did he . . . is he . . . leaving town or anything?"

She furrowed her brow. "No, he's not leaving. I'm still going with him. Why?"

"Well, it's just that I know Jack is dying for you to ask him, is all."

Lily's look of confusion deepened. "I told you, I'm going with Kyle. Remember?"

"Yeah, I just wasn't sure." My desperation was rising. "I mean, I just didn't want you to rule out Jack.

He's really great and stuff. And you hardly know Kyle. I just thought—"

*"You just thought you like Kyle too! And you don't want me to go with him!"*

I looked at her quickly. But she was staring down at her sneakers. I knew she hadn't said the words out loud.

But I had heard them.

Lily dropped her bag and turned to face me square on. "Listen, Sara. I know you said you weren't psyched about asking Jayden. But I thought you didn't want to because you were just shy. I didn't know you had a problem with me asking Kyle. Is it because you like Kyle too? If that's the case, why don't you just be honest with me?"

My stomach clenched up. She had it all wrong. With a shock of horror, I realized I'd forgotten all about telling her I'd asked Jayden. We had had a pact. I'd promised her I'd tell her the second I asked him, and I'd broken my promise.

"No, Lil, it's not that at all!" I said quickly. "In fact, I meant to tell you—"

"Hey, dudes," said a voice behind me. It was Jayden.

I had never been less happy to see him. The timing was just awful.

"Hey, Jayden," said Lily with a distracted smile.

"So, what do I wear to this shindig, anyway? Is it coat and tie, or can I wear normal clothes?" he asked me. "What do they mean by 'semiformal' on the posters?"

I darted a look from Jayden to Lily. Her eyes widened with surprise. And then a look of hurt crept into them.

"Oh, uh, I think it's a little fancier than normal," I stammered. "Like, a tie or something."

"Cool. I can handle that. Got to run to practice before Coach makes me do sprints for being late!" he said, and hustled down the hall.

The tension between us was thick. My best friend, the only real friend I'd ever had, was mad at me.

"Lily. I'm sorry. I totally forgot to mention that I asked Jayden. It's just that I've had a lot on my mind lately—"

"*Yeah, what's been on your mind lately is how all you've been thinking about is yourself. We had a promise! How could you forget?*"

Now I was officially freaked out. I'd been looking straight at her. Her lips hadn't moved.

"It's fine. Really," said Lily, this time out loud. "That's great that you guys are going together. But I have to run or I'll be late for dance. I'll see you tomorrow." And she hurried away down the hall.

I leaned against the bank of lockers. I had blown it big-time. I didn't have a lot of experience with having a best friend. I had even less experience having a best friend *and* trying to keep spirits from harming her. I'd certainly flunked this friend test. Best friends told each other stuff. Best friends didn't promise to do something and then not do it. I thought about the first time I'd seen Lily. She'd been outside her house, playing with her little brothers. I remembered how I'd liked her right away. How I'd wished I could be part of her life, her family, wrapped in her positive energy. Now Lily would probably never speak to me again.

What I wanted to do was lie on my bed and mope. Feel sorry for myself. All I could think about was Lily and how I'd messed everything up. But I made myself open up my closet.

I had to stop obsessing over Lily and Kyle. And the spirit in the next room. I had to start behaving like a normal twelve-year-old girl and think about what to wear to the dance. Wasn't that what normal girls did?

I stood in front of my closet, glumly looking over the few dresses I had hanging there. Each one was all wrong. The too-summery, too-flowery thing I'd worn last June in California, to a wedding of a colleague of my dad's. The dress I'd worn to the Harvest Dance—I was pretty sure it was a major fashion faux pas to wear that dress again to this dance. The too-small-for-me, too-little-kiddish Christmas dress I'd worn to a school concert two years ago. I sighed. The last thing I wanted was to ask my dad to take me shopping at the mall.

I heard my dad clear his throat softly behind me. "Whatcha looking for, kiddo?"

"Something to wear to the dumb dance on Saturday," I mumbled in reply. "I keep thinking I'm going to find the perfect dress in my closet. And then I remember that I don't *have* a perfect dress. And how much I hate shopping."

I expected him to look alarmed, like a deer in headlights, at the mention of shopping and dresses.

But he totally surprised me. He grinned. "Come with me. I might have an idea," he said.

Feeling slightly bewildered, I followed him up to the attic. Most of it was filled with old stuff that had belonged to Lady Azura. I wondered if she'd ever thrown anything away. An old dressmaker's dummy, a sewing machine, several huge trunks—the kind people used to take on ocean voyages. They were stuck all over with stickers, advertising exotic ports of call. I remembered that Lady Azura had done a lot of traveling with her late husband, Richard.

There was an old-fashioned-looking couch with a spring boinging out of the seat, and a bunch of paintings stacked against one another along one wall. There was a jumble of antique-looking lamps and clocks and other mysterious and interesting-looking stuff draped under sheets. This would be a fun place to explore, I told myself. But not in the winter. It was unheated and freezing.

In the spacious, cedar-lined storage room, my dad pulled the string on the overhead light and then moved aside a couple of boxes of Christmas decorations that had been piled on top of a big trunk. I'd seen the moving men carry the trunk up to the attic on the day we moved in, but I'd been so preoccupied by having just arrived from California to a strange new place that I hadn't really paid it any attention.

He tilted it on its side, so it was standing vertically on the floor. It was almost as high as my shoulder. He flicked the clasps and opened it up. Inside, a bunch of garment bags were hanging on padded hangers.

"These were your mother's," he said. " I held on to them for you, to give them to you someday. I don't know if they'll be any use to you for this dance of yours. . . ." His voice trailed off, and he cleared his throat. "But she was pretty into clothes, and she always looked great without seeming to try."

I saw his Adam's apple bob up and down.

"You're nearly as tall as she was now," he went on, his voice sounding a little huskier. "Anyway, have a look. Maybe there's something here. But if not, just let me know and we can go to the mall. Okay, kiddo?"

I felt my eyes get hot. My vision misted up. "Thanks, Daddy," I said, taking a small step toward him.

He enveloped me in his arms.

And then he quickly dropped his arms and left me alone. I heard him thud down the attic stairs.

I stepped over to the trunk and unzipped each of the garment bags one by one. Some of the dresses seemed really fancy; they looked elegant enough to wear to the Academy Awards or something. A few others were pretty, but they looked too grown-up for me to wear to a school dance.

I unzipped the last garment bag and looked at the dress. It was short, periwinkle blue, and simple, with a halter-style neckline. It was hard to tell what it would look like on. I pulled out the hanger, teasing the dress away from the garment bag. It couldn't hurt to try it on. I found myself wondering where my mother might have worn it. Maybe to a photography opening?

I held the dress to my face. Closed my eyes. Took a deep breath. Did I detect a faint smell of perfume? I kept my eyes closed, breathing in the scent of my mother's dress from so long ago. Trying, desperately, to conjure up her face, her smile. Her image appeared to me, but it was the one I knew by heart, the image I'd stared at in my favorite photo of her. The one of her sitting on a rock with her knees drawn up to her chin, smiling.

I opened my eyes. I had to stop trying so hard, trying to see my mother, whose spirit never visited. I knew I'd get really upset really fast if I thought about it for too long.

I hung the dress on the knob of a cabinet while I closed and reclasped the trunk. Then I brought the dress downstairs. As I passed my dad's room, I peeked in. He was sitting in his chair, reading one of his mystery novels. Although I wasn't so sure about the reading part. It looked more like he was staring into space, thinking. Probably about my mother.

I brought the dress into my room and hung it in my closet. This was enough effort thinking about the dance for right now. I told myself I'd try it on later.

The next day, Thursday, I started feeling panicky. Like I would not find Kyle in time. It was bad enough that Lily and I were fighting. I still had to try to protect her, no matter what she thought of me. I walked home from school by way of Scoops, so I could peek in and see if Kyle might be in there. I had to find him before Saturday. I had to tell him the truth before the dance. Although I had no idea exactly what I was going to say and how I was going to say it. But he wasn't there. Again.

When I opened the door to my house, the first thing I heard was shrieking and wailing. This startled me. The spirit rarely made that much noise during the day. All thoughts of Kyle flew out of my head.

Lady Azura was standing in the foyer, one hand on the newel post, the other clutching and kneading her lace handkerchief. She and I looked at each other. Her gaze was steady but grim. The lights flickered on, off, on, off, on again. We both stood, listening to the wailing spirit.

"My hearing may not be what it once was, but even I can hear that," Lady Azura said dryly. "She's been doing this all afternoon."

I dropped my bag on the floor and looked up the stairs.

"Your father is home early." She gestured with her chin toward the basement door. "He's down checking the circuit box. Again."

I heard my dad coming up the stairs. He emerged into the foyer, looking deeply uneasy.

"Sara," he said, "I don't know what's going on. But

I don't like the way the power is acting. I—"

We heard a crash. The splintering of glass. My dad and I both jumped about a foot in the air. Lady Azura seemed to have heard it too, because she turned around and looked up the stairs.

It had come from the pink bedroom.

"Stay here!" my father shouted at me. He took the stairs two at a time.

I moved to the foot of the stairs and listened. Lady Azura stood next to me.

"Was that a window breaking?" I asked.

"My ears are not what they should be," she said. "But I believe it was."

"Did—did *she* break it?"

"That is entirely possible."

I heard my dad calling to me. He was telling me to bring up a broom and dustpan. I scurried to the kitchen, and then raced upstairs to the pink bedroom.

"What happened, Daddy?" I asked in a small voice as I handed him the broom.

He began sweeping. I stooped down to hold the dustpan for him.

Three panes of glass had shattered and fallen into the room.

"Be careful," he warned. "Don't touch the glass with your fingers."

Ignoring what he'd just said to me, he stooped down and began picking up the larger pieces and putting them into the wastebasket he'd dragged over.

"Could it have been a tree branch or something?" I asked hopefully.

He paused in his cleaning and looked at me. "Doubtful. The tree is too far away to have done this, and anyway, there's hardly any wind."

I nodded.

"I want you to stay out of here," he said, taking the dustpan from me and dumping the remaining pieces into the wastebasket. "It's not safe."

I stood up and walked out of the room, feeling his eyes on me. I knew he took my silence as agreement. I hadn't promised, though.

Lady Azura was still standing at the bottom of the stairs where I'd left her. I paused halfway down and let my father pass me on the steps. He was carrying the

wastebasket and the broom and dustpan. He passed
Lady Azura without saying anything. He headed for
the kitchen, and we heard him rummaging around in
there.

"I'll be back!" he called. "Running to the hardware
store!"

We heard him open the door, hop into his truck,
and drive away down the driveway.

"What do you think just happened up there?" I
asked Lady Azura.

"The spirit is more troubled than I have ever seen
her," she replied. "Perhaps her aura caused a strange
vibration and broke the window."

"Could it be something else? Something other than
the weeping woman's spirit?" I asked tentatively.

Lady Azura seemed to grow agitated at my question. "Of course not," she snapped. She must have seen
the surprised look on my face, because she paused a
moment before continuing, this time in a softer voice.
"It's her, Sara. I just don't know what has caused her
grief to become this strong so suddenly."

"I have to find out. I have to get her to talk to me."

She sighed. "Your powers are strong. You can do so

much, but you have more to learn. You cannot force her to talk to you, my child."

I lifted my necklace out of my shirt and fingered the green tourmaline. "I have to stop her from doing bad things, Lady Azura, whether she's doing them on purpose or not," I said. "I have to try. What if he decides the house isn't safe? What if he wants to move out? I won't leave, Lady Azura. I can't." My eyes filled with tears.

She crossed her arms and frowned. "Let's not worry about things that might be, and focus on things that are. As for the spirit, I wish I could help her. I have tried several times over the years, but she is unwilling to open herself to me. And I'm too old to climb the stairs."

"I'm not," I said. My fears about the prospect of leaving were making me brave. "I'm going to go talk to her. You just said yourself it must be her. We know she's not malevolent. I will talk to her. I can help."

Lady Azura seemed to stare off into space for a few moments. I could tell she was considering very carefully what I had just said. It made sense. I knew she agreed with me. Finally she spoke. "I will not try to stop you. You must follow what your heart tells you to do. But be careful."

I wondered briefly if Lady Azura's granting me permission to talk to the spirit somehow offset the fact that my dad had forbidden me from entering that room. But I knew it didn't. I'd be breaking my dad's rule, something I hated doing. He asked so little of me.

But this was too important.

# Chapter 10

The door to the pink bedroom was slightly ajar. I entered quietly.

The room was freezing. The wind blew in through the open panes, making the bed ruffle ripple. The pages of an old magazine on the bureau flapped.

The spirit sat in her chair, crying, rocking. She looked solid and alive—much like Kyle. And just like with Kyle, if I hadn't seen the air rippling around her, and felt the familiar nausea rising in my stomach, I might have thought she was a living person, except for the old-fashioned dress she was wearing.

She stopped sobbing. Rocked. Stared out at the bay, across the steel-gray water in the fading light of the February afternoon. Large tears glistened on her pale cheeks, and every so often a low moan escaped her. Dust motes danced in a ray of sunlight, which beamed onto the faded bedspread.

I moved quietly over to the window seat, which curved below the base of the window, and sat down facing her. She didn't look at me. She just kept rocking back and forth. Her chin quivered. Her dark eyes looked anguished.

"Um, hello," I said.

She acted as though she hadn't heard me, but I was pretty sure she had. She buried her face in her ghostly hands, her long, tapered white fingers clutching her head, her thin shoulders shaking with grief.

I plowed on anyway. "My name is Sara. I've come by a few times, but we've never really talked. I hear you crying a lot. I am so sorry about your little boy."

More weeping. But now I felt as though she was listening to me, at least a little. Because her sobbing grew quieter.

"What was his name?" I asked gently.

At first I thought she wouldn't answer. But I waited. And then she pulled her hands away from her face and spoke.

"Angus," she said. "His name was Angus."

"That's a nice name." *Now what?* I thought. She was looking at me, expecting me to say something more. So I pressed on. I wasn't sure what to say, but the words started tumbling out.

"I know what it's like to lose someone," I began. "My mother died right after she had me. I never knew her. But I miss her. I look at her picture all the time. I look a lot like her. My dad told me she wanted more than anything to have a big family. And that she was beautiful."

The spirit took her face out of her hands and looked at me, her eyes wild, her mouth contorted. There was so much energy radiating off her, but I realized none of it was scary energy. She wasn't going to harm me. I was sure of it.

So I kept talking.

"I just thought, maybe, if you wanted to talk to someone, you could—"

Suddenly the light in the room dimmed. At first I thought the spirit was affecting the power again. But that wasn't what was happening. The world seemed to tip, and then right itself.

Warm sunshine poured into the room. A summery

breeze wafted gently into the room, stirring the lacy white curtains that now hung in the window, which was no longer broken and patched up. The patched wallpaper was now intact, the pink-and-blue floral pattern bright and clear.

I could see in a flash that it was summertime. The green lawn was dotted with bright-yellow dandelions. Hydrangea bushes burst with heavy blue blossoms. I could make out the street in front of the house. It wasn't paved, but instead had a strip of green grass running down the center of it.

The woman sat in the rocking chair, her hair swept back in a dramatic and complicated knot on top of her head, her beautiful emerald dress clasped at the throat with a sparkling brooch. In her arms she held a baby, wrapped in a lacy white blanket. Next to the rocking chair stood a handsome man dressed in an old-fashioned-looking topcoat with tails, close-fitting gray pants, and shiny shoes.

The spirit was showing me a vision.

I looked around the room. The furniture all looked the same, but newer. The carpet was bright and colorful. On the dresser stood a big bowl with a pitcher inside it.

I gazed at the young family. The baby—Angus, I assumed—wore a white cap on his head. Golden curls peeked out beneath the cap, and his huge blue eyes stared up at his mother adoringly. The three of them looked so happy, bathed in that golden sunshine and filled with such pure love for one another.

Then the scene faded away, and we were back in the room with its dim, February light. The spirit sat in her chair, quiet now. She rocked back and forth and looked at me.

"Thank you," I said softly. "Thank you for sharing that memory with me."

She nodded. And then she spoke. "Have you a family?" she asked me softly.

For a second I wondered why she was asking. I mean, we'd been living in this house with her since last summer. But then I remembered what Lady Azura had told me awhile ago, that spirits don't necessarily pay attention to the living. At least, not the way you might think they do.

"Yes, I have a family, although it's a pretty small one," I said. "My father is still alive. And he and I live here, in this house, with my great-grandmother from my mother's side. She lives downstairs. I didn't grow up knowing my great-grandmother, but now that I do, I—we really get along great."

The spirit nodded, her head down. "That is good. It is good to have family, family that you care for deeply. Nothing is more important than family. They can make even the terrible things bearable." She looked up, and for the briefest moment our eyes met. She gave me a small smile.

She began to fade. I could see the back of the chair right through her.

And then she disappeared.

I sat there for a while, listening to the old, ticking clock on the wall and staring at the empty rocker, which still rocked ever so slightly. Had I helped at all? I wasn't sure. But she *had* smiled. Maybe that was a good sign.

I left the pink bedroom and went to my own room. I pulled out my favorite picture of my mother. No wonder my dad looked at me funny sometimes. I could see the look in his eyes, how much I must resemble her. I stared at her blond hair, her smiling eyes. I stared at it for a while. I knew every part of the picture. I'd looked at it a thousand times.

My thoughts turned to Kyle, and what I was going to do. What *could* I do? How would I find him? Even if I knew how to summon a spirit—which I didn't, at least not like Lady Azura could—I was pretty certain I couldn't summon a spirit if he didn't realize he was dead.

I held my green tourmaline crystal, rubbing it between my thumb and finger, thinking, thinking. A plan was starting to form in my mind. A crazy plan.

# Chapter 11

That night I didn't hear the sobbing spirit at all. The lights didn't blink. I actually had my first decent night's sleep in a couple of weeks. I wondered if I really had made a difference.

Toward morning, I had a dream. I was sitting in the backseat of a car. We were driving somewhere sunny and tropical. We passed palm trees and a sparkling blue ocean. A kid sat next to me. A boy. He was dressed in a baseball uniform. The two people in the front seat seemed to be a mother and father. They were playing some jazzy, old-time music, and all three were singing to it at the top of their lungs. I laughed, because they seemed so happy. And then I woke up.

For the first time in days, I woke up feeling refreshed and ready to get out of bed, even before my

MP3 alarm had gone off. Maybe tonight I'd plug my clock radio back in, I told myself. That would be the real test of whether the spirit's energy was still short-circuiting stuff. It was nice to start the day having had a happy dream. I smiled, in spite of all the worries I was having about Kyle and Lily.

I lay there in bed. I thought about the idea I'd had last night. It seemed just as good in the light of day. Better, in fact.

I would conjure Kyle's parents. Who better to break the terrible news to him than his own parents?

The question was how to do it. I had doubts about whether I'd be able to handle this situation by myself. Should I ask Lady Azura for help? She'd forbidden me to get involved with Kyle. If I did ask for her help, and she said no, then I'd really be in trouble. She'd be watching me closely, overprotectively, and I might blow the one chance I had to fix things before the dance tomorrow. But I hadn't told her the whole story, especially the situation with Lily. Much as I loved and wanted to obey my great-grandmother, Lily was my best friend.

At school, I thought about it all the way through

art and assembly. I thought about it during lunch, sitting with Lily and the rest of my new group of friends. Just as the bell rang, ending the lunch period, Jayden approached me.

"So what time should I come by tomorrow?" he asked.

"Oh!" I said, surprised. "You're going to pick me up?"

He grinned. "My uncle has a sick new sports car," he said. "And he's visiting from college for the weekend. He offered to chauffeur us."

I smiled. I personally couldn't care less about cars, but I knew a bunch of boys in my grade were borderline obsessed with them, and Jayden happened to be one of them. "Sounds great. Why don't you come by at seven?"

"Cool," he said.

I made one last attempt to find Kyle on Friday afternoon. He wasn't in Scoops. But Lily was.

As I peeked in the window, I saw her, sitting at the counter, talking with Dawn Marie. I hoped maybe they hadn't seen me, but Dawn Marie waved right away. I waved back, just as Lily turned around to see who was there. We looked at each other. I could see hurt and confusion in her face. I hesitated for a second, wondering if I should go in and say hello. But I was too worried about finding Kyle, fast. I waved at her one more time and kept walking.

I fretted the whole way home. I should have stopped! I should have gone in! Was our friendship over? If it was, it was all my fault.

By the time I got home, I'd decided I really needed Lady Azura's help. I went straight to her fortune-telling room and peeked my head in.

My heart sank. The room was all set up. She was clearly expecting a client. I smelled incense burning. Her conjuring bell was set out in the middle of her table. It could be an hour or more before she would be available to talk to me. I was starting to feel panicky about how little time I had left before the dance the next night.

She emerged from behind the heavy velvet curtain, looking like a fortune-teller straight out of central casting. She wore a pink silk headscarf, a flowing magenta-colored blouse, belted at the waist, over a magenta, orange, and aqua-patterned skirt that looked like something an Indian princess might wear. On her tiny feet she wore high wedge heels in a darker shade of magenta.

"Sorry to bother you," I said. "Looks like you're expecting someone."

"I am," she replied brusquely as she moved her conjuring bell to a different spot on the table.

"Should I—ah—come back later?"

She regarded me sternly. Had I upset her? I seemed unable to please anyone right now.

"What did you want to see me about?" she asked.

"I—I wanted to ask you if you would help me," I began. "I have a friend. A good friend. Who is in trouble, kind of."

She nodded, her large, honey-colored eyes regarding me steadily.

I swallowed. "I know that you love me, and that you care for me and are just looking out for me. And I also know that we're family, and families should help each other. But the friend I'm worried about is Lily. She's like a sister to me. And she needs my help."

She hadn't cut me off so far, so I kept going.

"I need your help conjuring a spirit. Two, actually. I

know you told me not to get involved with Kyle. But I have to. I'm worried because Lily is supposed to go to the dance with him tomorrow, and if they go, people might recognize him and he might, like, flip out if it suddenly hits him that he's not alive anymore. And I also feel bad for Kyle. He's a lost spirit. He needs my help too."

Her stern look vanished. She smiled and reached out. Took my hand in both of hers. "Those are very good reasons," she said. "You are teaching me new things about the spirit world, and the responsibilities that come with our gift, every day." She gestured toward the summoning bell. "I was expecting you, of course." With that, she gracefully fell into a chair beside the table and pointed to the other one, indicating I should sit too. "The family name was Parker, was it not?"

I nodded, filled with amazement. "Yes. Cecily and John. You mean, you set all this up for me?"

She nodded. "I owe you an apology. I was so worried about protecting you, I have kept you from exploring your true potential. I'd been against your helping Kyle because he is an unpredictable spirit, and beyond my control. I felt I couldn't protect you, and I feared for your safety. But I see now that my job is to help you develop your powers to their full potential. Only by helping you follow that path to move away from me can I hope to keep you close to me and safe."

She'd used the words "move away from me." Why had she made that choice of words? Was my dad planning to make us move? I didn't want to be the reason for a disagreement between him and Lady Azura. But I also didn't want to leave.

"I can see that you're worried about what your father will think," she said.

I nodded, not sure what to say. It always freaked me out a little when Lady Azura seemed to know exactly what I was thinking.

"He and I have had a long discussion about you. He is very concerned for your safety, of course. But he wants to do what is best for you. We have agreed that I can continue to help you. Let's leave it at that for now, shall we? One can only worry about so many things at a time, Sara."

She lit a large white candle and set it in the center of the round table. Then she turned off the overhead light. With the heavy shades drawn, the room was nearly dark.

We sat down across from each other, staring into the candle flame. I put my hands on the table, palms down, my fingers slightly spread. My heart thumped and my throat went dry.

"Block out all thoughts except for the Parkers," she said. She began humming and swaying a bit.

I bowed my head and tried hard to concentrate. I thought about Kyle. I thought about the dream I'd had last night, the good one. I was sure it had been a dream about the Parkers. I tried to remember what his parents had looked like in my dream. The memory was too fuzzy. And they'd been sitting in front, where I hadn't been able to see their faces clearly.

Lady Azura picked up her summoning bell and shook it gently four times, each time toward a different corner of the room. Then she spoke, her voice low and husky.

"Cecily and John, we are here. We wish to communicate with you. Do you know that we are present? Can you give us a sign that you are here?"

At first nothing happened. I could hear my own

breathing. I watched the flickering candle. The smell of spices—cinnamon, cloves, something else I didn't recognize—became fainter.

I started to lose hope. They weren't coming.

Then the candle blew out. The table began to shake, very slightly.

And then the candle relit itself.

I felt a chill begin deep within me, growing rapidly until the tips of my fingers felt like ice, and my toes, too. My breath grew shallow, as though a great weight had been placed on my chest. I closed my eyes. Tried hard to keep concentrating. Willing the Parkers to appear.

The table stopped shaking. I opened my eyes. I saw something swirly and gray in the corner of the room near the huge, carved-oak sideboard.

Two translucent figures, a man and a woman, had materialized. As I watched, their outlines became clear, but their features were hazy and indistinct, their eyes just black darkness. The man was tall, and he wore glasses and a long winter overcoat. The woman was petite and pretty, dressed for going outside in a belted coat and fashionable-looking high-heeled boots.

Kyle's parents. The people from my dream. I was sure.

Lady Azura spoke. "Thank you for joining us," she said.

I noticed she wasn't looking in their direction. Could she see them?

"Sara and I have been eager to speak with you."

She was looking over at the opposite corner of the room. Should I say something? I decided against it. I didn't want to scare them away.

"We are here," said Mrs. Parker in a faint voice.

Had Lady Azura heard her? I knew her hearing wasn't very good, but she seemed to. Her head turned toward where the spirits were actually standing. But I still wasn't sure if she could see them.

"We asked you to join us today," said Lady Azura, "because we would like to talk with you about Kyle."

Mrs. Parker let out a soft moan. Mr. Parker shook his head sorrowfully.

*"Kyle!"*

The word had been whispered, but it seemed to bounce off every corner of the room, and it echoed. I couldn't tell if it had been a male or a female voice, but I had heard the sadness in its tone.

"We believe he is confused, and needs your guidance," said Lady Azura.

I blinked. Mr. and Mrs. Parker began to fade. I felt a wave of panic. They couldn't leave, not yet. Not before we'd had a chance to ask them to talk to Kyle.

I looked at Lady Azura. Her face was calm; her eyes unfocused. The spirits were right near her! I was now fairly certain she couldn't see them. I had to say something before they left.

"Please!" I said, my voice sounding high and sort of strangled.

I didn't look at Lady Azura, but I could feel her tense up across the table from me. But I kept talking. There was too much at stake.

"I see Kyle around a lot," I said. I had no idea if I was using the right words. "And he—he doesn't know that—that he has passed on. He thinks he's alive. He is really nice and stuff, but he doesn't belong here anymore. I am so worried about what he might do when he finds out the truth. It's only a matter of time before he does, because, see, he's been hanging around with other kids and they can see him. Can you talk to him? Can you explain it to him?"

Mr. Parker sighed. "We will try."

Mrs. Parker just shook her head. Then she whispered, *"Kyle. My boy."* But this time it was a quiet whisper. I wasn't even sure if Lady Azura had heard her.

Lady Azura spoke up. "Thank you for trying," she said. "He deserves to be at peace."

They shimmered in and out of focus. On some level I knew it was only moments before they would leave us.

"Wait!" I begged. "Please don't go yet! You see, there's kind of a time issue with all this." I swallowed and then kept going. "See, tomorrow, there's a dance? And he wants to go? And his cousin Tom is going to be there. And it would be kind of a disaster if Tom saw Kyle, you see, because . . ."

I could barely see them now. The oak side table materialized behind them.

"We will try," whispered Mrs. Parker again.

And then they were gone.

Lady Azura spoke up. "Thank you, John and Cecily. Sara and I—"

"They're not here anymore," I said in a small voice.

She sniffed, then pulled out a lace handkerchief and dabbed at a spot on the crystal bell.

The silence between us felt thick.

"Was that, um, okay that I spoke up?"

She hesitated. Then she nodded, her lips tight. "Yes, I suppose it was. I am old, and my powers are fading. Yours grow stronger every day, and you are gaining confidence. Still, a conjuring can be a delicate balance. Spirits are unpredictable."

I swallowed hard and nodded. I hoped I hadn't offended her. It was hard to tell sometimes.

# Chapter 12

Saturday morning. The day of the dance.

I stared across the breakfast table at my dad, wondering why he was looking at the apartment rental section of the newspaper. I kept staring, waiting for him to say something, but he was too engrossed in the ads. Finally I couldn't take it anymore.

"Dad, why are you looking at apartment rentals?" I asked. I hadn't intended for my voice to come out as shrilly as it did.

My dad put down the paper and sighed. "I'm just looking, kiddo. But to be completely frank with you, I am beginning to wonder if perhaps we ought to move. I don't think it's safe here. I—"

I couldn't believe what he was saying. I don't usually lose my temper, especially with my dad, but I couldn't stop myself. "You moved me here!" I shouted, cutting him off. "You made me leave California. You kept the fact that Lady Azura was my great-grandmother a secret for months. You kept all kinds of secrets that I had a right to know. And now, when I'm finally feeling good, and happy, and I finally find out I have a great-*grand*mother I didn't know I had, you want to take it all away from me? That is not all right. You can't do this to me, Dad."

His blue eyes suddenly got all glinty. Was he *crying*? My *dad*? This could not be happening.

"Sara. I lost your mother. I can't lose you."

Now a tear actually spilled over the bottom of his eye and rolled down his cheek. I was too shocked to say anything. All the anger I'd felt moments ago melted away.

"If something happened to you, I'd never forgive myself. I'd die."

I had never seen my dad cry. Never. And somehow I'd caused this. Part of me wanted to jump up and throw my arms around his neck. But the other part wanted to throw myself on the floor and kick and scream like an angry toddler.

Here's what I ended up doing: I ran out of the room, up the stairs, and into my bedroom, where I threw myself on the bed and cried.

I spent most of the day in my room. I didn't want to talk to my dad, or to Lady Azura. I spent several hours working on my collage, and then I turned on my computer, listlessly scrolling through my friends' postings about what they were wearing that night, who liked whom, which people were going as couples, who had broken up with whom. I just didn't care. There were no texts or messages from Lily.

Early in the afternoon, I heard my dad's truck drive away. Knowing it was Lady Azura's naptime, I crept downstairs and into the kitchen and made myself a turkey and pickle sandwich, even though I didn't have much appetite. Then I tiptoed back upstairs, climbed under my covers, and fell asleep.

When I woke up, the light in the room told me it was late afternoon. I looked at my clock. Five o'clock!

I hauled myself out of bed and checked my phone. Nothing from Lily, but Jayden was confirming that he'd be by for me at seven. I halfheartedly texted him back, telling him seven was still good.

I realized with horror that I'd never tried on my mother's dress. I'd been so preoccupied that I had forgotten all about it. I pulled it out of my closet and looked it over. It was definitely around my size. But it was one of those kinds of dresses that are really hard to tell if they'll look good or bad until you try them. I kicked myself for not trying it on before. I looked grimly at the too-summery, too-small, too-fancy dresses hanging in my closet and quietly prayed this one would look half-decent. If not, I'd be wearing the Harvest Dance dress again.

I took a hot bath and washed my hair. I don't usually do much with my hair—just wash and go—but Lily had given me some beach spray stuff a few months ago that she said would make my hair wavy. I spritzed some on my hair and then blew it dry the way I'd seen Lily do, with my head upside down. I used my fingers to tousle it instead of using a brush. The end result, I must admit, was pretty nice. My hair looked wavy, like I had just spent the day at the beach.

And then it was time to get dressed. I pulled the dress off the hanger and slid it over my head. At first I thought it would be too big, but the dress fit me practically like a glove. I walked over and looked at myself in the old, somewhat smoky-looking mirror in the corner.

I blinked at myself. I looked good. The dress was perfect. The neckline was halter-style, and it made my shoulders and arms look, well, graceful. And the blue matched my eyes exactly. I wondered if that was why my mother had bought it. Because it had matched her eyes too.

Then I saw something else in the mirror. It was something white, flickering behind me. I turned.

The spirit of the wailing woman was sitting quietly on the end of my bed.

# Chapter 13

"You look so lovely," she said softly.

"Thanks," I said.

This was the first time I'd seen a spirit here, in my room. But I didn't mind it. I hadn't felt any of the usual signals telling me I was in the presence of a spirit—the tingling in my foot, the nausea, the feelings of dizziness.

I wondered if this was the first time she'd emerged from the pink bedroom. Was this a breakthrough moment for both of us?

"This dress belonged to my mother," I told her, smoothing it down self-consciously as I turned to face her. "I wasn't sure it would fit okay, but it does, right? Fit okay?" I asked shyly.

"It does," she confirmed for me. "Your mother

would be very happy to see you looking so lovely in her dress," she added.

I walked toward her. "I don't suppose . . . you wouldn't by any chance . . . know her? Natalie Collins?"

The spirit shook her head.

The brief surge of hope I'd felt vanished. Of course she wouldn't know my mother. This spirit had been stuck in this world, in the pink bedroom, for the past eighty years.

I was trying to think of something to say next when I heard a voice calling from down the hall. It sounded like a child's voice, a happy voice.

Had I heard the word "Mama?" I wasn't sure. But then, as I watched, the spirit rose up from the bed. She turned toward me with a little smile and drifted out of the room.

I knew what I had heard. Her child. Calling to her.

I went downstairs a little while later. My primping was done. I'd put on some makeup, something I didn't do very often. Just a little mascara and some pink lip gloss. (The gloss was another gift from Lily. The mascara I'd actually bought myself.) I'd dug out my one nice pair of shoes—black sling-backs I'd worn to the Harvest

Dance—and was relieved to find that they seemed to look good with the dress. I felt pretty klutzy walking in them, since I usually wore sneakers. But if Lady Azura could do this every day, I could do it for one night. And besides, I could kick them off once I got to the dance.

I heard my father and Lady Azura talking as I tottered into the kitchen, but my father broke off mid-sentence when he saw me. He stared at me.

Lady Azura stared too. But she seemed to recover a lot quicker than my dad. She moved across the kitchen and grasped my hands.

"Sara, you look beautiful. So much like your mother."

She reached out and tucked a strand of my hair behind my ear.

I smiled shyly.

"You do, kiddo," said my father. His voice came out low and husky.

*She really does look just like Natalie.*

I looked up at him. He coughed and looked away. He hadn't said that out loud. He picked up his magazine and hurried out of the kitchen.

I checked my phone for the zillionth time. Still no word from Lily.

I left Lady Azura sipping her tea in the kitchen, a faraway look in her eyes. I went out to the front hall and paced. Now that the excitement of getting ready for the dance was over, I was overwhelmed with worry. Where was Lily? Was she with Kyle? What if Kyle's parents got to him just as he arrived at her house?

My phone vibrated in my hand. It was Jayden.

ON OUR WAY. BE THERE IN A FEW.

I hadn't seen Kyle since we had conjured his parents. Had they reached him? Did the spirit world even work that way? What if they didn't get to him in time?

I knew what I had to do.

I quickly texted Jayden.

I'M SO SORRY. I CAN'T DRIVE THERE WITH YOU. SOMETHING CAME UP SUDDENLY. WILL MEET YOU THERE IF I CAN.

I thought about all the arrangements Jayden had made, getting his uncle to drive us in style in his cool car. Now there was a chance I wouldn't even make it to the dance at all, if I couldn't find Lily.

There was no immediate reply from him. I was sure he would have gotten the text—he'd said he was on his way.

Great. So now I'd managed to anger not only my

best friend, but also the guy I had the world's biggest crush on. Neither one would probably ever speak to me again.

I pulled off my shoes and hurried toward the front door, where I shoved my feet into my clunky snow boots. *So much for being careful with hair and makeup,* I thought, hearing the gusting wind outside.

I had my coat and gloves on and was reaching for the door when someone knocked. I pulled it open, and a gust of wind whooshed into the hallway, sending a pile of junk mail flying.

It was Jayden. He was all dressed up. I could see a tie peeking out from beneath his coat. He was smiling. Happy.

My heart sank. He hadn't gotten my text. I looked over his shoulder at the car idling in the driveway. It was a shiny red sports car. I could see his uncle in the driver's seat, banging rhythmically on the steering wheel and bobbing his head up and down, as though listening to raucous music.

"Oh! Hi!" I said. *Now* what was I going to do?

He looked at me curiously. "Hi," he said. "Why do you look so confused? Do I have the wrong night or something?"

"Oh no, it's just that, well, I sent you a text."

"Oh. Thought it was my mom, telling me to be home on time." He pulled his phone out of his pocket and looked at the text. His brow furrowed.

"Ah," he said.

Obviously it was my turn to say something. I knew I should explain. But there wasn't time. I had to get to Lily fast. Anyway, how would I explain this to him?

"I'm sorry," I said. "I have to go see someone right away."

"Soooo," he said slowly, "you're . . . maybe . . . not even going at all?"

He was annoyed. He tried to mask it, but he was annoyed. At me.

"I don't know," I said miserably. "I hope so. I'll try."

"Okay," he said shortly. "Well. See you around, I guess."

And he turned on his heel and trudged down the steps.

I watched him get into the car. He slammed the door a little too hard. He said something briefly to his uncle, and the car drove away down the driveway.

He would never speak to me again, that was for sure.

I closed the front door. I leaned against it, breathing hard. Then I snapped out of it.

Lily. I had to help her if it wasn't too late.

I had my hand on the knob, ready to head outside, when someone knocked.

I flung open the door.

It was Lily. Her cheeks were streaked with tears.

I pulled her inside without a word and threw off my coat.

"Sorry, were you just leaving?" she asked in a quavery voice.

"I was on my way to see you," I said.

She nodded.

"Did something happen with Kyle?"

She nodded again.

I waited, in horrible suspense.

"He left me a note," she said. "In our mailbox. He said he was going home and couldn't come to the dance. Just like that."

I put my arm around her and pulled her close. She put her head on my shoulder, sniffed once, and then lifted it again. I could see she was back to the old Lily.

"I mean, talk about tacky," she said as she pulled

off her coat and threw it next to mine. She was back to her normal tone of voice. "Who writes *notes* anymore? Does he think it's 1980 and texting hasn't been invented? I mean, I gave him my cell number and everything. I so don't buy the going-home-suddenly thing. I just saw him yesterday, and he said flat out he had no plans to go anywhere, that he was going to be hanging around Stellamar indefinitely." She rolled her eyes as she took a moment to breathe. "He probably has a girlfriend back in Florida, and she probably found out about the dance, and he was probably too chicken to tell me. Whatever."

I smiled at her. Lily was going to be fine. "We'll have fun anyway," I said. "Jayden told me that Jack is going to be there, and he doesn't have a date or anything, and that he was really sad when he heard you had asked someone. Just saying."

She raised an eyebrow interestedly. I loved the way she could do that. I'd tried in front of a mirror a few times, but I just couldn't get my eyebrows to cooperate. Then she looked at me, as though noticing for the first time. "Wow, Sar. You look amazing."

"Thanks. This dress was my mom's."

"You look like you just stepped out of an old Hollywood movie, and I mean that in a good way."

"You look beautiful too," I said, and meant it. She had on a peach-colored sleeveless dress with a tight bodice and a full skirt. Her dark hair was piled up on her head, and the cut of the dress perfectly suited her slim, dancer's body.

"Thanks. This dress was dumb luck," she said, flipping the skirt out with both hands but looking quite pleased with herself. "My cousin Kim gave it to me. It was a designer sample that came to the store and she got to keep it, but it didn't fit her. She is way into clothes, and she told me she thought it would look perfect on me, and it did fit pretty well."

"Should we go, then?" I asked. "I'm sure my dad will drive us."

"I thought you were going with Jayden."

I shook my head. "We're, uh, not really exactly going to the dance together anymore. He's a little, um, mad at me about something."

Lily gave me another huge hug. "Well then, I guess we'll go together, you and me. Boys, schmoys," she said, stepping back and tugging her dress back into place.

I gave her a rueful smile.

"I'm sorry I got mad at you, Sara. You had a feeling about Kyle, I could tell. You knew he was bad news, and you tried to tell me, but I didn't want to hear it."

"I didn't think he was bad, Lil. I just didn't think he was totally right for you," I babbled. I was so filled with relief that everything had worked out and that Lily wasn't mad at me.

"From now on, I'm going to listen to you when it comes to boys!"

"Lil, really, I have no clue how to talk to boys," I protested. "I'm terrible at flirting and stuff."

She shrugged. "Maybe so, but I think you have a sixth sense when it comes to reading people's personalities. I'm sticking with your judgment from now on."

My dad poked his head down from around the stairway landing. "You girls need a ride to the dance?" he called.

We looked at each other and both smiled. "Yes, please, Dad!" I called back to him. "You must have read our minds!"

# Chapter 14

I hardly recognized the gym when I walked into the dance with Lily half an hour later. The place was transformed.

Sparkly white lights had been hung all around the walls, and there were a bunch of small round tables, draped with lavender tablecloths. A long table near the seating area was set up with drinks and snacks. Everyone was dressed up—even the teachers, who stood around the edges of the room, chatting with one another.

Up on the stage, a real band was playing, an old-fashioned kind of band with old-school musicians wearing sparkly jackets and bow ties. The music was old-fashioned-sounding, but fun all the same. It made you want to kick off your uncomfortable black sling-back high-heeled shoes and get out on the dance floor and dance. I reminded myself glumly that I'd ditched my date and probably wouldn't dance at all that night.

Jack came charging up to us. I almost didn't recognize him in his jacket and tie. Like most of the boys there, he wore big high-top sneakers. But somehow, the look kind of worked. The thick part of Jack's tie was a little shorter than the thin part, which I was pretty sure wasn't the way it was supposed to be, but he looked cute anyway.

"Hi!" he said, staring at Lily. "You made it!"

Lily smiled. "Yeah, we got a little sidetracked, but we made it."

"You guys look awesome," he said, staring straight at Lily.

"So do you," said Lily. I nodded politely.

"Tied my own tie," he said proudly.

"You don't say," said Lily.

"Do you want to dance?" He was, of course, looking at Lily.

Lily looked at me, and I nodded. "Go!" I said, giving her a little shove.

She and Jack made their way through the crowd and onto the dance floor.

So there I was, standing all by myself. Great.

I decided to head to the bathroom to hide for a while. Then I noticed Jayden standing ten feet from me, staring at me.

He crossed his arms and looked away.

I crossed my arms too and shivered. Swallowed hard. Then I walked straight over to him.

"Hi," he said, scuffing his sneakers and looking down at the floor.

"Hi," I said. "Listen, I'm really sorry I couldn't drive here with you. Lily needed me, and I just had to be there for her. I feel terrible that I wrecked your plans for the car ride. I hope your uncle wasn't too upset."

That had to be the longest speech I'd ever uttered to a boy in my whole life.

Jayden looked up at me. "No big deal," he said with a shrug. "I just wasn't sure if, well, if you wanted to go with me at all. I thought maybe, I don't know, you decided to go with someone else."

I should my head quickly. "No! Believe me, that is so not what it was about."

He grinned, that amazing, sweet, sideways grin of his.

I could see in an instant that he wasn't mad anymore.

"Cool," he said. "That's a nice dress. You look nice, I mean." I could tell he was nervous. That somehow made me feel way less nervous. Our eyes met, and we both laughed. "So you want to dance? Get something to drink? Maybe shoot some hoops together?"

I laughed again. "In these heels I could probably dunk it. But nah. I guess I'd rather dance right now." I leaned down and took off my shoes, then added them to a line of others near the wall. I guess a lot of people had had the same idea.

He took my hand and led me out onto the dance floor. The band had taken a break and a DJ was filling in. The DJ, a kid from Stellamar High, was playing a song I recognized from the radio that was easy to dance to. I'm not the most confident dancer in the world, but the music made it easy to forget about that and just move to the beat. That was what we did.

Lily and Jack were dancing right near us, laughing and talking to each other. Nearby I saw Dina Martino and a tall, good-looking boy with brown hair and green eyes who looked a lot like Kyle. It had to be Tom, Kyle's cousin.

And then my eye was drawn to a dark corner of the gym, near a bunch of band equipment. Something luminous was moving around. It was the spirit of the gym teacher. He was dressed in his usual ill-fitting polyester tracksuit. But he was moving his feet to the music and appeared to be enjoying himself. I smiled.

The next song was a slow dance. Jayden cocked an eyebrow at me, and I nodded. We drew close to each other, and I put my arms around his neck. I breathed in his smell, almond soap with a hint of pine needles. I leaned my cheek on his shoulder.

Something caught my eye. I raised my cheek and stared over Jayden's shoulder at another luminous image.

Three spirits shimmered. Kyle was standing between his parents. Could everyone see them?

"What's the matter?" asked Jayden. "You just got all clenched up."

I relaxed again. Kyle didn't look the way he had when I'd first seen him. He looked less solid, more spiritlike, his image flickering slightly, like an old film.

I saw Marlee and Avery walk right past him without a glance.

They couldn't see him.

Kyle was smiling at me. His father's hand was on his shoulder, his mother's hand was tousling his hair. As I watched, the three spirits faded and vanished.

*They must have come here to say good-bye to me,* I thought. I smiled and closed my eyes, listening to the music and breathing in the scent of Jayden, my first-ever actual kind-of boyfriend.

*"I don't know how to do this. To tell her."*

My eyes flew open. That had been Jayden, but he hadn't said it out loud. I was hearing his thoughts somehow. I had no clue how I was doing it. I waited, tense. Was he about to break up with me before we'd even actually officially gone out together?

*"How do I tell her that my family is moving back to Atlanta next month?"*

# Want to know what happens to Sara next?

Here's a sneak peek at the next book in the series:

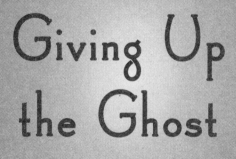

# Giving Up
# the Ghost

Snowflakes swirled around me as I clenched my arms against my middle and shrugged my shoulders, shivering in my thin T-shirt, blue jeans, and sneakers. The wind whipped my hair around my face, but I was too cold to reach up and tuck it behind my ears. My body shook. My teeth chattered. Why hadn't I worn a coat?

I worked my half-frozen fingers into my front pocket, searching for my Christmas list. But my pocket was empty. I scuffed my sneaker through the powdery snow in frustration and immediately regretted it. Snow quickly soaked through the thin canvas of my sneakers, sending fresh shivers up and down my spine.

Holiday shoppers bustled past me on the busy

street, laden down with packages and looking warm and happy, bundled up in their parkas, wrapped in scarves, cozy in their knit hats. The shops along Beach Drive were brightly lit, twinkling with lights and decorated with Christmas stuff. Again I wondered why I was outside with no coat on.

Then I saw her.

The crowd seemed to part like curtains. She stood alone on the sidewalk, wrapped in a fancy-looking winter coat. Her head darted back and forth like a bird. She looked nervous. Wary. Suspicious. I'd never seen her before, yet I couldn't shake the feeling that she was somehow familiar to me.

She was a very strange-looking woman. Her eyes were the color of antifreeze. She had thin lips and a long, hooked nose. Her hair was snow white, but her smooth skin made me wonder if she was old enough to have white hair. She could be anywhere from thirty-five to sixty-five. Maybe she was one of those people, I thought, who have had such a sudden, nasty shock that their hair turns white overnight.

And then, as if someone had just turned up the volume on a radio, I heard her thoughts.

*. . . can't take this . . . get away from the crowd . . . that way, that way . . .*

Followed almost immediately by the thoughts of everyone else who was passing by.

*. . . get that scarf for Uncle George? . . . Did I send a card to the Nelsons? . . . The flight gets in tomorrow morning . . .*

They were all just snippets. Fragments.

I had been able to hear other people's thoughts for weeks now. Not always. And not everyone. But it was happening more and more. This was a new power. To add to the ones I already had.

I'd been able to see spirits—dead people—for as long as I could remember. Recently that power had intensified, and for a while now I'd been able to interact with the spirits, to talk with them. Since I'd arrived in Stellamar last summer, I had gradually come to accept these powers. Before moving here, back when I lived in California, I'd hated them. They made me feel different, and I just wanted to be normal. But with my great-grandmother's help, I was actually starting to look on them as the "gift" she insisted they were. Most of the time, anyway.

But this new power was different. I wasn't sure I liked being able to listen in on what people were thinking. Sometimes you heard things you wished you hadn't.

Now my head was pounding—the thoughts of multiple passersby crowded inside my head, bouncing around inside my brain and practically deafening me. It was like someone tuning a radio, from station to station, rapidly and on high volume. Or like being in a very crowded, noisy room with terrible acoustics.

Suddenly I realized that the strange woman could also hear people's thoughts. Because she jumped when people passed by, as though their thoughts grew louder, the way they were doing in my own mind. And she looked as though she hated this scrambled, deafening noise as much as I did.

The woman hustled across the street, weaving her way between shoppers. She scurried under the huge sign that announced the Stellamar Boardwalk. Ignoring my instincts, which were telling me to run, not walk, as fast as I could away from the woman, I followed her. My feet seemed propelled by a will of their own.

As I emerged onto the windy, weather-beaten

boardwalk, I saw her leaning on the railing and look-ing out at the slate-gray, choppy waters. Curling wisps of snow tumbled and danced between us. We were the only ones. No one else in their right mind would willingly stand there, bearing the full brunt of the icy December wind off the ocean.

The woman didn't notice me. She seemed way too absorbed in her own thoughts, staring out at the ocean. Now I could hear her thoughts clearly, because they were no longer mixed up with the thoughts of all the other people.

*Must stop . . . Can't do this anymore . . . Why? Why did I not stop when I had the chance?*

As I watched, a scrap of paper fluttered and swirled around the woman in an erratic figure eight on the whirling wind. It hovered gently in the air in front of her, like a butterfly about to alight on a flower. As if in a daze, she plucked the paper from the wind and stared at it.

I was at least ten steps away from her, but I could clearly see what it was. A copy of one of the fliers my best friend, Lily Randazzo, and I had made last sum-mer. We'd made a bunch of them to help advertise my great-grandmother's business and hung them all over the boardwalk. LADY AZURA! PSYCHIC, HEALER, MYSTIC.

The woman stared at the paper. I heard her thoughts.

*Lady Azura is still in business? Well then, I will go to her. I will make her help me.*

She seemed to know my great-grandmother. Maybe I should approach her. Offer to help. But something stopped me. She seemed angry. Hostile. And what did she *want*? Suddenly I felt wary. Protective of Lady Azura.

My teeth began to chatter. From the cold or from my fear, I wasn't sure. But probably both.

She folded up the paper and shoved it into her coat pocket. I had just decided that the best thing to do would be to run the other way when she wheeled around and faced me. Bored a hole through me with those eerie green eyes.

I forgot all about how cold I was. My heart pounded in my ears. I felt as though that green, probing stare was hypnotizing me. Like it was drawing me toward her, and I could fall in and drown. She was so strange-looking. Not old, not young. Fierce. Determined-looking. I thought about running home to warn Lady Azura that this weird woman might be showing up.

She tilted her head back and laughed. "Weird woman?" she said in a mocking voice. "You want to warn Lady Azura that I might be showing up? That is an excellent idea. But there's nothing she can do. *Nothing!*"

She'd heard my thoughts. Read my mind.

"The damage has been done!" she said, pointing at me. "The energy has been released."

Now I was officially freaked out. I turned to run away. Fast. I ran. Tripped and fell.

And then I woke up.

I was in my darkened bedroom. I was all twisted up in my sheets. My hair was plastered to my forehead with sweat. My heart was thudding like a big bass drum.

I managed to kick away my covers. I sat up and looked at the clock. My mind was groggy. It felt like the middle of the night. But the clock read seven fifteen. Why was it so dark in my room? It was too dark to be past seven a.m. on a morning in March. For a moment I had the strangest thought, that there was a cloud in my room, hovering over my bed. I stared up into it and tried to make sense of how this was possible, wondering if I was still asleep.

After closing my eyes and opening them a few more times, I realized it wasn't dark in my room at all. It was a bright, sunny day. The window was open. I could smell the fresh sea breeze blowing off the ocean. I could hear birds twittering, and smell coffee brewing. The darkness in my room had been my imagination. It had to have been. It was a beautiful, sunny morning. Not a cloud in the sky, let alone one in my bedroom.

I swung my legs around and got out of bed.

That had been one weird dream.

check out these other

great series from

Simon Spotlight . . .

You're invited to a

# CREEPOVER ™

Published by Simon Spotlight • KIDS.SimonandSchuster.com

MARTONE SAYS
SCHOOL YEAR OFF
TO GOOD START

upside ran down to it.
Why are naut niors out?
um a rain sorcero ever
with ending owns, to be

elyrandya
before
Mildewist
um e loo
overtim